Escape From A Nightmare

By Stephanie Acon

P.O. Box 2535
Florissant, Mo 63033

All Prioritybooks titles are available at special quantity discounts for bulk purchases for sales promotions, premiums, fund-raising, institutional or educational use. For information regarding discounts for bulk purchases, please contact Prioritybooks Publications at 1-314-306-2972 or info@prioritybooks.com you can contact the author at: scacon007@yahoo.com.

Edited by: Lynel Washington and Kendra Koger
Cover Designed by: Sheldon Mitchell of Majaluk

Library of Congress Control Number: 2011938371
ISBN: 978-0-9834860-2-2

First Prioritybooks Printing: September 2011
10 9 8 6 5 4 3 2 1

Printed in the United States of America

A Special Acknowledgment

(MUST READ)

First, I want to thank God, and his Son, Jesus Christ, my Lord and Savior. Although I completed this novel prior to my commitment to Him, I owe all my highest praises to Him for hearing my prayers and blessing me. I thank Him for the measure of faith which He has supplied and increased in me; for I have received because I believed, and ONLY because I believed. I thank my pastor, Michael Grady, for agreeing with me, according to the Word of God, for the releasing of my book. *(Matthew 18:19 ~ Again I say unto you, that if two of you shall agree on earth as touching anything that they shall ask, it shall be done for them of my Father which is in heaven.)*

This book was written from my heart and the observations therein. I am truly grateful for my many gifts, including this talent for writing, which was blessed unto me as a child. It was given to me because I asked, and believed.

I thank my publisher, Rose Beavers, for joining her faith with mine. Our faith is in God the Almighty, not the economy! You are my first publisher, and I truly thank you for being a part of God's plan for my life. I believe that success is not only in the making, but already established, appointed, and DONE. Just hold on, and whatever you do, DO NOT EVER DOUBT...ONLY BELIEVE. Our testimony will be great.

I thank my mother, Beverly Poole, for her support and I thank my father, Karl Acon, for his creative genes.

I thank Systematic Muzick Inc.—Stephen "Instrumental" King, Carlos Minor, MC 923, Lo Lansky, and KD Assassin—you guys are my label mates…my FAM…my friends. All of you mean so much to me in unique and individual ways. However, collectively, it is because of your belief in my skills as an artist, and leadership that I gained significant confidence amongst my peers. Others saw the light later, you saw it from the beginning. You handed me a microphone, and allowed me on the stage to speak before the crowds. Then on top of all of that, you all saw me as much more than a "female" rapper. You saw me as a force to be reckoned with before anybody else got the memo. *And you let it be known!* Nobody was messing wit' it! Y'all believed, and that's why I was put down on the team—*O.E.S.C and The Murc Unit. (Let me reiterate, it was you - Stephen, 923, Lansky, and Los - who proved to me your real love and loyalty for me was not just music, but authentic in life. It's so funny how we meet and bring so many people into our world, but God has a way of bringing the original back full circle. When I needed true friends and love, you continued to call and check up on me. You were genuinely excited with me and for me as you watched me switch gears. You kept it 100! And I thank you. I had to learn the hard way that some people were not my friends…they were fans. Now I know the distinction, and will not confuse the two again. Real friends show you with their actions, not just their lips.)*

Finally, I thank the Hip-Hop generation.

I thank you for teaching me raw confidence and creativity. Always respecting me, and my style, always accepting me no matter how many levels up I drifted, and continue to drift. Life is an experience, and a dream indeed. I learned that from YOU. You have never mocked me— only admired me. You have never closed an eye on me; you have only held open your nose for me. When I went hard, you went wild! When I fell back you sought me. I know you are listening…and watching…so here's to YOU.

Enjoy…and learn something!

4

Dear Hip-Hop generation,

It is true. We were indeed, once lovers. And because of that sincere love for one another, we promised that we would never turn our backs on each other. You believed in me, and I believed in you. You were there for me for a moment, and I was there for you for a season. Although I had to move on, I have NOT forgotten you. I left to find the truth...and bring it back to you.

~ Stephanie Acon

a.k.a

NinaRaw

Escape From A Nightmare

Prologue

Tall houses surrounded the large pond. There was a great distance between them, but somehow, they all appeared together. He watched her through the upstairs window. Her hair was thick and curly, but the strands were disarrayed. The dress she wore was a dingy white. She sat before the pond with bare feet curled at her side. She intrigued him.

Slowly, he approached her from behind. The cold air caused the pond to release a steamy mist that blended with the surrounding fog. He wanted to touch her, but he did not want to frighten her. So he stood. Then, he looked up to the dimly lit sky. The sun peeked through one great hole amongst the clouds. It appeared a million light years away.

He then lowered his head to look at her. She stretched out her legs before the pond and was about to place her bare feet into the freezing water. "Stop!" he shouted.

He thought she would turn completely around, but she didn't. She only slightly turned, exposing the side of her chocolate-brown face. He noticed the dimple as she smirked. With her legs still outstretched, she dipped part of her feet into the water.

"They're going to freeze and it's going to hurt," he said to her.

She replied, "It won't hurt, this is just a dream."

"No, it's not a dream." He felt the labored breathing within his chest.

She spoke again. "How can you tell a dreamer what is a dream and what is real?"

Before he could answer, she turned her face forward and dipped the rest of her feet into the water.

"Stop, please!" he shouted in vain.

He watched in horror as she then slipped her entire body underneath the water.

Hesitant at first, he moved forward to the edge of the pond where she once sat. When he glanced down into the water, she was gone.

Chapter 1

Jannette screamed through Gabriana's cell phone. "Fo' real, that's how you wanna be? You're playing yourself."

"Mama, please stop yelling. It isn't like that, I'm grown."

"You are hardheaded and you never listen," Jannette continued on. "You're selfish and you only think about Scholar. It's all about him in your narrow mind! And what about Milan and Ciona? You don't hang with them anymore, and matter of fact, you don't even really mention their names!"

"That's because we are all grown and I don't have to hang around them like I'm twelve!" Gabriana was more than heated now.

"You know what, Gabri? You are wrong and I can't believe you... You are a terrible friend. You aren't real. Real friends don't change. God doesn't—"

Before her mother could complete that last sentence, Gabriana slung the BlackBerry across the room, smashing it into a wall. She pushed Cobi's head away from between her legs where she was seated braiding his long hair. She stood, grabbed her coat and headed for the front door.

"Man, what are you doing? My game is in an hour and I need you to finish my head," Cobi pleaded.

"Shut the hell up," Gabriana hissed as she stormed out onto the front porch, slamming the door hard.

The freezing rain and flurries mixed in the air, melted all around

Gabriana. She felt as if her ears were on fire. Throwing on her hood, she sat on the top step and fired up a cigarette. It wasn't really the conversation with her mother that had caused her explosion. That was more like the last straw. Gabriana was already on the edge from the altercation between herself and her boyfriend, Scholar. About thirty minutes prior to her mother's call, he had smacked the hell out of her in his upstairs bedroom. She was still stunned and boiling with anger.

"It wasn't even like that," she whispered to herself while inhaling the cigarette smoke.

It all began when Scholar stepped into the bedroom. Pulling his T-shirt over his head, Gabriana reached up to help him adjust himself. He was a very handsome dude with a blemish-free, perfect caramel baby face. A deep-waved Caesar cut cropped in low rows covered his head, and muscle-toned rips traveled up his medium-built frame. Scholar's firm arms were coated with unique tattoos and popping veins. His eyes were slit like small almonds, with a slight droop about them, and were still bright and lively. They always seemed focused and attentive. Gabriana never could determine which of Scholar's features drove her the craziest. Was it his eyes, his soft nose, or the soft lips attached to his charming smile? She loved him and appreciated his physique wholly. Scholar was indeed a "new" kind of gorgeous. Sexy. He stood about five-foot-eleven, but in heels, Gabriana was around five-foot-nine, threatening his position in height. Leaning forward to tap her lips against his, Scholar stared into her glossy eyes.

"A'ight, what's wrong with you?" he'd asked her.

"Nothing, baby, I'm straight."

"Nah, girl, I know you and something is bothering you," Scholar said as he moved quickly around the room.

12

Gabriana hesitated with the details that had been on her mind all morning. Just as he was about to let it go, she briefly described the dream. Last night Gabriana had another one of her disturbing dreams. Scholar stood with his back to Gabriana, while digging through the top drawer of his dresser. After she finished telling him about her dream, she approached him slowly.

"So what do you think? That dream was crazy, right? I mean, it scared the—"

WHAMM!

Before Gabriana could finish, Scholar turned around and smacked stars into her vision.

"I told you before, don't ever bring nothing else like that to me. I don't wanna hear none of that," he screamed on her.

Gabriana was in total shock. Yeah, she had seen Scholar angry plenty of times, and he had smacked her a few times on other occasions, but never with the force she felt this time. Before she knew it, she lunged forward and tried to grab at his face, or anything, but he grabbed her around her neck and threw her backward onto the unmade bed. Gabriana reached on the nightstand, grabbed a half-can of strawberry soda and threw it at him. Red fizzle splashed recklessly. Scholar looked down at his stained clothes, swooped forward, grabbed a handful of her thick hair and yanked her head backward. He then moved in as closely to her face as he could, and with gritted teeth said, "I will break your neck up in here. It's not a game with me. The next time you speak a jinx on me, you are gone, and that's on everything I love," he threatened.

Scholar released Gabriana and walked into his closet. After removing his ruined shirt, he grabbed a brand new T-shirt and his black casual Prada coat then exited the room. Within ten minutes, he left the house without her.

As Gabriana sat there on the step, she thought about the dream, then dismissed it. "I need to never open my mouth about my stupid dreams again. People don't understand them. I need to just learn how to keep my mouth closed," she said aloud to herself.

After tossing the devoured cigarette, Gabriana still didn't move. She thought about her mama, Milan and Ciona. They all used to be so close. Gabriana was an only child, so her two best friends were as close to siblings as she could wish for. They had been friends since what felt like forever. Gabriana missed them dearly, but not enough to fit them into her new lifestyle. Scholar and his family had captured her full attention and they kept her thoroughly entertained, especially Scholar. He lived the life. The house where his mother and two siblings were residing belonged to him. Scholar was a known dude. Not only was he getting money in the streets, he was also the local "hoodstar." He earned fans and followers because he hustled, he street-balled on the basketball circuit, and he got down in the rap game. On top of all of that, Scholar's father was "that nigga". Gangster. Feared.

His father, who preceded him in street fame, had earned another breed of respect. He was a cold-hearted, no-nonsense man, who was serving life for everything from extortion to murder. The reputation of Jacobi Jamison, Sr., was impeccable in legend, so Scholar had already inherited respect just on general purpose. Although he wasn't as grimy as his father had been, he was definitely a go-getter. The people seemed to love him for that alone.

Gabriana and Scholar had been an official couple for almost three years now.

Gabriana didn't have much family around, except for Jannette, so Scholar's mother and father, two siblings and his many friends caught

14

Gabriana up. Her mother was very dear to her, but since Jannette had given her life to the Lord the previous year, things weren't quite the same for the two. Gabriana and her mother had been extremely bonded, and before Jannette's transformation, the two could have been mistaken for friends. Hanging out and talking about everything, the mother and daughter were inseparable until Jannette's conversion. At that point, she really became a *real* mama and she would consistently drill her daughter. She loved her so much that she wanted the two of them to be together for eternity. When Jannette tried to explain this, Gabriana wasn't feeling any of that talk. The new pressure her mother put on her caused her to throw herself into her love, Scholar. Before anyone knew what happened, it was too late. It was now all about him and his. Mama went straight to the back-burner, and friends, well, Gabriana figured that she could get back up with them whenever she felt like it.

Finally beginning to feel the reality of the wind, Gabriana made her way back into the house.

"Where did Cobi go?" she asked Scholar's older sister.

Toree was a tall, lighter and thinner version of her younger brother. The brown freckles on her slim face contributed to her distinction.

Toree sat in front of the TV then lit her blunt before responding, "Girl, don't even worry about it. Mama is upstairs, finishing him up right now."

Gabriana removed her coat and tossed it onto a nearby chair. She then took a seat next to Toree and reached out for the blunt.

Passing the stuffed cigar over, Toree asked, "What the hell did you say to my brother earlier? That nigga stormed out of here, going off."

"Who, Scholar?" Gabriana asked dumbfounded.

15

The look that Toree gave her said it all.

Gabriana hit the blunt back to back, then toked it a couple more times before responding, "Nothing. Absolutely nothing."

She paused and then continued, "And if it was something, you do not want to know, trust me."

Chapter 2

It was almost midnight.

Scholar, Brick and Gabriana sat in the black-on-black Escalade, smoking their third blunt. Gabriana was seated in the back because she was still angry at Scholar for smacking her the day before. During his absence, he had not bothered to call her and he hadn't answered his phone when she had tried to call him. Scholar had not returned home 'til almost an hour ago.

When Gabriana saw the truck finally pull up, she hopped from the porch were she was posted, smoking her square. She climbed into the backseat. With much attitude in her tone, she asked, "Where you been?"

Gabriana anticipated an explanation, but Scholar ignored the question and continued his conversation with Brick. Once the blunts were rolled, the passing around began. Gabriana began to relax and was soon on her level. Now, she sat quietly, listening to the two guys talk.

"It's all or nothing, fam. Once I lay the ink on that paper, I'm securing the whole scene. Ain't nothing or nobody getting cuts unless they go through me," Scholar boasted.

"That's my goal fo'real…I'm the King out here or I'm nothing!"

Brick hit the blunt and never released the smoke. He spoke and said, "Scholar it's done. Ready or not, this world better be prepared for you." He then stalled his point as he began to choke uncontrollably. Scholar started laughing and patted his boy on the back. Brick continued, "I mean, as long as you stay real, and as long as you feed your niggas, I got your back *one hun'ed*. Just keep it real and get this money because that's all that's about to matter. Get the label de—"

"Man, what," Scholar quickly replied. "Nigga, what do you mean 'about' to matter? This *is* all that matters to me right now and everybody better recognize that. My movement is definitely number one on the agenda. Straight-up."

Gabriana tripped off of Scholar's little selfish remark, but to be honest with herself, she didn't really care. She had been down with Scholar for the last few years and she accepted how cocky he could get when it came to his music. Scholar was just a cocky individual, period. It came with the territory, and the position. He was a local celebrity and Gabriana was well-aware of his ambitions of bigger stardom. She ignored his ego because she just wanted to see her dude make it, and for sure this nigga was taking her along for the ride. He had already told her countless times how he was going to make it. Knowing the power of words, thanks to her mama's teachings, she believed him one-hundred percent; now, it was all happening. His dreams were now obtainable. Gabriana was proud to believe that she played a part in all of that. Despite all his grinding, Scholar's big breakthrough came when Gabriana met and passed on an elite connection of hers to his manager. That crucial contact put Scholar's resume into the right hands, and the rest became history. Everyone was eager to make the star shine globally.

Sometimes Gabriana would think about the groupies who would come along with his stardom. How would he handle them? How would *she* handle them? "Whatever, I ain't no insecure chick," she would tell herself.

Gabriana was a pretty young lady, unique in her own right and pushing the age of twenty-eight. She had cocoa-brown skin with deep dimples, just like her mama. She possessed signature jet-black eyelashes and thick naturally curly hair that stopped just past her shoulders. She had only recently begun to flat iron her hair straight, thanks to Scholar. He actually liked both hair textures, but would often ask her to straighten it out just to see if she would do whatever for him.

Scholar was an extra-tender thirty years of age. His advantage was his baby face and surely his management would sell him to the world as much younger. His music consisted of raunchy street talk and club materials. At the time, Gabriana loved Scholar so much that to her, as well as his legion of supporters, he was nothing less than "the one".

Gabriana sat in the backseat, staring forward at Brick. He was a thick, muscular dude with brown skin and Caesar waves just like Scholar. By his own nature, as usual, he was scowling as he talked. Brick kept an attitude, but when he did smile, which was rare, he would make anyone around him smile. Gabriana appreciated this about him, however, she did notice a red flag. Brick seemed to smile a lot more often when the two of them were alone and talking. Unlike how he acted when Scholar was around, Brick would always smile when dealing with Gabriana. Whenever she would notice this, she would just brush her suspicions off.

Gabiana turned her attention from Brick back to Scholar who was seated directly in front of her. She loved to look at her dude from any angle. She began to gently rub the back of his head in a soothing manner. Scholar held back any acknowledgment of her gesture and kept his focus on Brick.

Gabriana smiled. "Yeah, okay," she said to herself.

No longer angry, she slowly crawled between the seats where Scholar and Brick sat, still gunning their mouths. Both dudes paused, mid-discussion, and stared at her in astonishment. She knew that she had interrupted their conversation, but who the hell cared? Not her.

With no regard for company, Gabriana straddled Scholar as if they

19

were alone. She kissed her dude on his forehead, then his nose, and finally his lips. When she finally caught his smile, she then closed her eyes and kissed him as if it was their last kiss. Brick stared for a moment then frowned before turning his head. The envy on his face was obvious, even if just for a moment, but neither Gabriana nor Scholar noticed it. They only saw each other and their future. The thoughts of Gabriana's dream from the other night faded from both of their minds, and at that second in time, *she* decided to never look back.

Nothing else matters, she thought to herself. *I know exactly who I want to be with— forever.*

Chapter 3

Two months later...

Gabriana was seated in the last row in the back of the crowded van. Everyone was facing forward. As she stared out the large window she thought to herself, There are so many people. Where are they all going?

Suddenly, a skinny kid jumped up and smacked the side of her window. Gabriana was startled out of her trance.

Bmmpp...

He smacked her window again...and then again. Gabriana just sat and stared at the little boy jump up. She was frantic, but her body did not move. Glancing over, Gabriana looked through the window to her right. Someone suddenly caught her attention.

"What in the—?"

Her heart felt as if it was about to explode. She screamed out in terror. "Stop this van...oh, my God, please...stop now!"

Gabriana slid over to her right and placed her face close to the glass. With both of her hands on the window, she stared out in disbelief.

It was Cobi. He was in a suit, standing outside on the church steps. So many people were walking the streets, but he stood there alone with his head down.

"Cobi, look up and come to me!"

Scholar's younger brother never looked up. Gabriana felt as if no one could hear her. She continued to scream until she was out of breath. She looked forward toward the people ahead of her in the van and yelled out again, "Please, turn around...stop, please!"

No one acknowledged her. Looking back toward Cobi and the front of the church, Gabriana watched helplessly as the casket was being carried up the stairs to the sanctuary. Strangely, all the people near and around the church all had on the same suits and were wearing the same facial expressions. As Gabriana stared through the glass, someone tapped her left shoulder, causing her to jump. When she glanced over there was a man seated next to her. He tried to speak, but Gabriana became overwhelmed and terrified with an anxiety she had never felt before. A shrilled scream escaped her throat and then she awoke.

Gabriana screamed and looked around the room. "Where am I? Oh, my God, help me," she wailed in a panic.

The hotel room was large and there were a few champagne bottles lying around. A couple of seconds later, Scholar emerged from the bathroom with a towel wrapped around his waist. There was a look of confusion on his face and he was soaking wet. "What is wrong with you?"

Gabriana looked at him with the same confusion on her face, but did not reply.

"Gabri, what is your problem? Answer me, why are you in here screaming like that?"

"I don't know," she answered. "It was...another dream." Gabriana mumbled, "It was so real."

Scholar just stared at her and then said, "Gabriana, the apple don't fall far from the tree, do it? Shake it off. Shake that psycho monkey off." He then retreated back into the bathroom and slammed the door.

A small painting on the wall fell to the floor.

Gabriana grabbed her hair and buried her face into a pillow. "I cannot stand you." Her muffled outburst vibrated the soft material surrounding her face.

She thought about how insensitive Scholar could be sometimes. Every since she was a child, Gabriana had been a dreamer. Since she was five years old, she would wake up in the middle of the night, screaming and crying. Her mother would always comfort her. She never judged or scolded her for the midnight disturbances. Why couldn't her man provide that same support? Gabriana could never confide in him about her dreams or how she felt about life's mysteries. He wasn't the type; he wasn't having it. Scholar rarely talked about anything other than himself, his goals, money or fame. His views on subjects such as God, Jesus, or any religions were simple. His motto was, *If I can't see it or feel it, it doesn't matter.* Once while at her mother's house and Gabriana was upstairs getting dressed for their date, Jannette had asked Scholar if he believed in God. His response to her was honest. "I don't know what I believe."

Jannette pitied him during that conversation. She replied, "Scholar, if you don't know your God, then you don't know yourself. You have to know God in order to love Him. You have to love Him in order to love yourself."

Scholar did not disguise his frown. He looked to the ceiling and exhaled frustrated air. When he returned his eyes toward Jannette's, both of their expressions of distaste met head-on.

She continued in a slow, deliberate tone, saying, "Ultimately, you cannot possibly love my daughter if you do not love yourself."

Becoming angered by her words, Scholar said to Jannette, "Look, no disrespect, but like my father told me a long time ago...I AM God."

Jannette was taken aback by this young man's arrogance. *Who would teach their son that type of nonsense? That's craziness,* she thought. However, she did not express those questions to Scholar. She simply shook her head negatively and told him, "You are not God. You are *not* the Father... nor his Son. You are a fool."

Scholar didn't reply to her. He got up from the large La-Z-Boy chair and left her house immediately without saying another word or even offering a good-bye. He was so offended that he left Jannette's front door wide-open purposely as a sign of disrespect. When Gabriana called him a few minutes later to ask him why he had left, Scholar told her that her mother had disrespected him. With a hint of hurt in his voice, he asked Gabriana, "Who is she to disregard anything my father ever instilled in me?"

Gabriana didn't understand what he was talking about. Her only reply was, "My mother is not the same and she is always tripping nowadays. Just let it go, baby." But he couldn't. Ever since that evening, Scholar secretly despised Jannette. He never felt that she liked him. Whenever Gabriana would bring him around her mother he would grow quiet and/ or agitated...and it always showed. Eventually, Gabriana stopped bringing him around her mother. Jannette didn't necessary disagree with this, but the catch was losing time with her daughter. Gabriana was *always* with Scholar.

The night before had been a celebration for Scholar's recent record-deal signing. Gabriana, Scholar and all of his family and friends had partied all night at three different clubs, all featuring personalities from the local hip-hop and R&B radio stations. It seemed like everyone in the city came out to support her dude. She was so proud of Scholar. Everything was finally happening, but it was all happening so fast.

After Gabriana and Scholar departed the hotel, Brick escorted the couple back to Scholar's house, so he could pack. He was headed for New York City to handle some business with the record label and his management team. During the ride to the house, Scholar explained to Gabriana that he had been asked to join a popular hip-hop tour. It was a last-minute decision, but because of his rising popularity amongst the industry, his label and management wanted to utilize the opportunity to promote their newest artist. There was no doubt in anyone's mind that Scholar was about to blow up very quickly.

Gabriana didn't take this news well. "Why are you just now telling me this and why are you not taking me?" she asked with a salty attitude. Scholar chose this time to give the news to Gabriana purposely. He was not in the mood to argue about this with her, so he used his friend as a calculated distraction for altering his attention. Immediately, he turned to face Brick and changed the subject. Gabriana was beyond pissed. Once they were back at Scholar's house, Gabriana met him in his room to talk. She asked Scholar again why he was playing her.

"Don't start with me, Gabri. I already explained the situation to you, so what are you tripping about now?" Scholar started out calmly.

"Excuse me, are you serious?"

Shoving him in the face, she continued saying, "What is the matter with you? I have been the one here for you on your come up. I got your foot in the door and now you're leaving me behind. Nah, nigga, that ain't happening because you completely have me—"

Scholar interrupted her. "Who are you talking to right now, huh? You need to check yourself and keep your hand out of my face." He was now yelling at her. "*My* talent got my foot in the door, so don't ever give your-self that credit. You're nuts if you think I wasn't breaking through even-tually...with or without your help. So don't ever say that to me, again.

It is what it is and you're not going with me this round, flat out. And another thing, don't start tripping with me, or disrespecting me, because I'll leave you behind crying fo'real." Biting down hard on his bottom lip, Scholar looked at her directly in her eyes. "Don't ever think you can't get the eraser," he boldly said.

Gabriana couldn't believe that he had just said that to her. The couple stared at each other without saying anything else. Gabriana tried to walk away, but Scholar stopped her. He grabbed her elbow and pulled her into his arms then spoke in her ear.

"Gabri, I'm sorry…but I mean every word. You're my girl and I got you, but if you start acting opposite of that then you can forget about it. I will keep it moving and replace that pretty face before you can blink a lash. Are you understanding me?" He looked into her stunned face.

After another second, he continued, "But I don't want that for us... because I need your faith right now."

Gabriana kept quiet as she turned her face slightly away. On one hand, this was her dude, and she understood him, and what he was say-ing perfectly. The look on his face told her that he was dead serious and this hurt her feelings. On the other hand, she could not believe he had just mentioned her faith. Faith that she never thought he'd considered her having. This made her believe that maybe he really did need her for something. Considering the dreams she had been having, maybe she could use the free time to hook up with Jannette, and possibly convince her to pray for her baby. She then glanced up into unblinking eyes.

With that same serious look on his face, Scholar asked her, "So, are we good? Let me know right now if you are going to hold me down or what, because I'm going to need you like never before."

Scholar swallowed hard after that latter statement.

Gabriana didn't reply immediately. She continued to search over the face of her man. For some unknown reason, there was an eerie vibe that suddenly covered the two of them. During that moment, Scholar's breathing became almost shallow. The hairs on the back of Gabriana's neck collectively stood. She did not know exactly what was happening, but quickly wanted to diffuse the tension from the air. She placed a gentle hand on Scholar's chest. He opened his mouth to speak, but she placed the finger of her other hand up to his lips. The room remained in silence. Gabriana released an aura of unsaid emotion from deep inside, and for the time being, her spirit calmed Scholar instantly. She leaned upward and kissed him gently on his nose and then his lips. "I got you for life," she finally told him. "I got you for life."

~ ~ ~

It was a little passed 7:00pm when Scholar left the house to head for the airport. Brick stood at the back of the black-and-white, custom-designed Mercedes Viano L4. At his feet sat several large pieces of luggage. The van's trunk was open and ready for loading, but Brick continued talking to the bronze-tanned female standing on the curb beside him. She wore overly-fitting jeans with a short leather coat. Her fire-red weave was pulled back into a 22-inch ponytail, and her lips sparkled with thick, nude-colored lip-gloss. Large bangles dangled from her ears and wrists. She had Brick's full attention. Scholar walked up closely behind the young woman then reached out to her backside. It appeared as though he was reaching to embrace her, but instead he gently began to squeeze around the small of her back.

Scholar knew that Gabriana was in the upstairs window watching. She always peeped out from somewhere whenever he left out. He was aware, but still massaged this woman from the behind until she and Brick acknowledged him.

The female turned her face sideways and smiled. This caused Brick to pause mid-sentence and nod his head to Scholar.

Scholar smirked a moment before speaking. "What, nigga?"

Brick bit the inside of his jaw and gazed up at the slightly hidden face in the window. "You ready to roll? Nya's gonna follow us and park her car at the airport," he said to Scholar.

"Ah, yeah?" Scholar replied to Nya, instead of Brick. He pulled her closely in by the waist. "Oh, yeah, you flying out with us? You following us around now or something?" he joked, placing his face near her ear.

Brick shoved the last bag into the trunk and slammed the trunk door down. "Nigga, get in the car. You act like your girl's not in that window. You crazy, nigga?"

Scholar didn't respond.

"Whatever," Nya cut in, releasing herself from Scholar's hold. "I'm going to my car. Don't drive all crazy," she said as she walked away from both Scholar and Brick, then back across the street.

Scholar remained mute. He just stared at Brick; the look spoke volumes. Brick climbed into the driver's seat, but Scholar stood still for a few seconds before moving. He couldn't believe the way his boy had just fronted. *Who does that?*

It took Scholar another moment of scowling in Brick's direction before he shook off the urge to snap. Once he opened the passenger's door to take his seat, he glanced behind him, then up toward the window, but there was no longer anyone there. His eyes quickly roamed to the other windows on the face of the house, but they too were all empty. Scholar cleared his throat and spat on the ground before finally getting inside the vehicle.

As they rode off, Scholar kept silent outwardly, but inside he began a one-way conversation.

I shouldn't have done that...but she's gon' have to get used to some things now. Fo 'real. She gotta step it up and she's gonna have to be down—fo 'real. This is about to be our lifestyle now. MY lifestyle now... besides—

Before Scholar could fully get into his thoughts, Brick interrupted them.

"Nigga, how you gon' push up behind Nya while Gabriana was up in that window? You knew she was watching, why would you do that? She should have come out swinging. That was disrespectful, dawg."

"Brick, mind your business."

"I'm just saying…"

"Brick..." Scholar uttered through gritted teeth. "Mind your business, a'ight. You're acting like my woman is your concern. Nah...don't do that, bruh."

Brick stole a glimpse of Scholar. His tongue began to sting as his teeth pressed down. He wanted to lash out on the guy next to him, but he caught himself. Brick looked over again. This time, he roamed a little longer over the side of Scholar's face. He took notice of how his home-boy's jaw was twitching. Despite his own anger, Brick decided in that instant to fall back and let it rest. *That's on him*, he thought to himself.

Brick reached down into the cup holder to retrieve the freshly rolled blunt and a lighter. Again, he glanced over at Scholar who was looking way too serious suddenly. *This nigga...*

29

Brick reached over to hand Scholar the blunt as a peace offering. Scholar eagerly accepted. He wasted little time blazing the tip up. Inhaling and exhaling out a thick and steady stream of smoke, Scholar slouched down in his seat. His thoughts spoke his disapproval. He couldn't fathom what would make a nigga check another man about *his* behavior. In Scholar's opinion, if the topic wasn't about cash, business, or sports then niggas needed to keep their mouths closed. His private life should never be discussed indirectly or directly, point blank. If Scholar didn't bring up certain sensitive subjects, then it was for a reason. Advice wasn't needed. The nigga Brick needed the rules embedded in his membrane, but later for that. Scholar was trying to get lifted.

Brick took notes through his peripheral view. To him, what he saw next to him, was a dragon. A nigga that after all their years of friendship could not really be figured out. So, therefore, to Brick, Scholar couldn't really be respected...not fully. He just didn't really get why the nigga did certain things. He'd known his boy since they were eleven; still, Brick couldn't piece everything together. But he never let Scholar know that directly. He knew that regardless of his faults, there was something about Scholar that drew people in. Brick had to give it to him, the cat was kinda talented, especially in charming people. Brick couldn't read into everything, but he knew his boy better than the average person who encountered him, and dude wasn't nothing sweet. Scholar could be extremely slimy in public and personal relations at times. At least twice a day, the dude succeeded in pissing someone off. Still, he received the undeserving love of legions. It wasn't fair, but it was what it was and it was time to capitalize off that. Scholar was a goldmine. Brick knew when a man was on his way to the top, he wasn't crazy. If he was going to eat with his brethren, then he needed to keep the homeboy as close as possible. So he had to stay down—and be cool. He would allow Scholar his time at bat and would have his back. That was a conscious decision. As long as the homie didn't play him, or become brand-new, Brick made the choice to place all bets on his longtime partner.

Chapter 4

It had been two weeks since Scholar had left for NYC. Gabriana decided to stay with her mother while he was away. Gabriana and Jannette shared a homemade lunch of Caesar salad and Italian-style ravioli. Together they ate and talked. As usual, her mother shared her opinion of Scholar, his family and his lifestyle. Gabriana let it enter one ear and exit the other. Jannette noticed her daughter's sudden disengagement and figured she disapproved of the conversation. Switching the subject, she then began to tell Gabriana about how much the Lord had been blessing her. Gabriana laughed to herself. *Lady, you are tripping. Everything around here looks the same. As a matter of fact, the only difference I've seen since your salvation is how you no longer have men knocking your door down. How lonely? That's sad."* As if reading Gabriana's mind, her mother ceased the discussion.

Gabriana looked up from her plate and looked into her mother's eyes. Something looked different about them. Gabriana stared harder. Jannette pretended not to notice her gaze. *My mother is aging quickly, what the hell?* Trying to shake off the uneasy feeling, Gabriana did her usual, she returned her attention back to her thoughts of Scholar.

"Mama, if I asked you for a favor, would you say yes? But...before you answer, please consider that it's very important to me that you say yes."

Jannette looked at Gabriana and said, "Speak, child. And for the record, there is no such thing as a favor between you and me. You're my child and I will do anything for you, as long as it's not crossing the line."

This is why Gabriana adored her mommy so much. It had always been like this with them. There was nothing that Gabriana could do that could ever change that.

Finally, Gabriana spoke again. "Mama, I want you to pray for Scholar."

"Why, Gabriana? Is he in some kind of trouble?"

Rolling her eyes, Gabriana replied, "No, Mother, he is not." She huffed. "And I don't know why, I just really want you to, okay?"

Gabriana stood from the table, removed their emptied plates, and took them to the sink. She began to run hot water over the dishes when she heard her mother softly say, "Gabriana, come here."

Gabriana stood still for a moment before turning to sit with her mother again. Jannette reached for Gabriana's trembling hands. She knew her daughter very well. Gabriana had not displayed shaking hands since she was a little girl. For a moment, the two ladies shared a knowing look. Neither of them spoke.

Jannette tried to break the silence. "Gabriana," she whispered.

Gabriana removed her hands from her mother's hold. "Mama, stop! Listen to me, okay?" Jannette was silenced. "Mama, I've been having some bad dreams." Jannette continued to sit there quietly. "I don't understand them or what they mean, but I feel nervous when I wake. Sometimes, some of those dreams make me feel terrified when I look at Scholar and…" Gabriana looked down, trying to conceal her watery eyes. "Mama, I love that dude so much, and I'm very strong and all, but I'm starting to feel that anxiety I used to feel as a little girl. Although in the dreams, I do not directly see Scholar. I still have a bad feeling that..." Gabriana began to rub her ears harshly as she concluded, "I don't know. I know I'm not making any sense right now, but please just pray."

34

Again, Jannette reached for her daughter's trembling hands. "Bow your head, baby." She began to pray aloud. "Lord, cover my daughter with your blood and your hand. Many things… and many people will come and go, but my Lord, no matter what happens, please take my child and reveal all things to her. Closing this prayer, we ask for your mercy over Scholar. Let Thy will be done. In Jesus' name…Amen."

When Jannette released Gabriana's hands, she saw her baby doing something she had not seen her do in many years.

Gabriana kept her eyes closed and cried. There was so much more that she wanted to say to God, but she just didn't know how to make the connection on her own. Gabriana finally opened her eyes when she felt her mother hugging her neck from behind.

"Mama, I just don't know what to do sometimes. If I ever lose Scholar in any way, whether it be to another woman or fate, or anything, I just don't think I would be able to go on."

Jannette could not believe what she was hearing from her only child's mouth. Inside, she asked God for wisdom. She then gently said to her daughter, "Gabri, your life is one as an individual. You have a sole purpose on this earth. Find out what it is."

Removing Jannette's arms from her neck, Gabriana stood to face her. "My sole purpose is to love my man. Point blank."

Jannette was floored. She simply walked out of the kitchen and took a seat in the quiet living room. She could feel the tears threatening to fall. *Lord, my daughter is very special. No matter how lost she may come off sometimes, please let Your will be done and not hers. Amen.*

Chapter 5

It was after 8:00 o'clock in the evening and Gabriana was bored. Her mother was in her room, reading her Bible as she did every night before turning in for bed. Gabriana sat in her old bedroom, thinking. She thought about what her mother had told her earlier. *You have a sole purpose on this earth. Find out what it is.*

Although she had basically snapped on Jannette for that remark, Gabriana only did so because within herself, she knew her mother was right. She never told anyone how she really felt about her own ambitions she had sacrificed for her relationship.

When Gabriana and Scholar first met, she was an elementary school music teacher with a Bachelor's degree in Education under her belt. However, she had studied musical arts all her life and was an inspiring songwriter and composer. The day all of that changed was when she met Scholar.

Gabriana was attending a late-night session at a large studio located in downtown, St. Louis. The following day was Thanksgiving, and school was out, so she had decided to take Brian Weber up on an invitation to come in and work with him on some material. Brian was a well-known producer. The two of them had been working on a demo for Gabriana. Although she had no desire to see the limelight, Brian had convinced her to join the music scene as a songwriter, and promised to help shop her work to industry insiders. That night was supposed to be a private session between her and Brian; however, he had received a call saying that some local rappers wanted to come through. Not wanting to turn down the extra money that they were offering for the unscheduled studio time, he obliged. Gabriana did not complain. When she heard the loud crew enter the building, she gathered her notepads, and other belongings, then headed to a backroom located far down the hall to continue her writing.

Alone in the room, Gabriana leaned up against the old-fashioned piano with a pencil in one hand and her notepad in the other. She was humming melodies to herself and jotting down the lyrics as she sang them.

I'll never forget the day I was reborn

You'll never know just what that meant to me

I was like a child caught up, alone in the storm

Then that day you walked into my life

Gabriana repeatedly hummed the lyrics, searching for the right words.

Then that day you walked into my life, was like the day my life re-formed

Removing her weight from the piano, she wrote down more lyrics then turned around. When she finally looked up from the pad in her hand, she became startled at what she saw. He frightened her because she did not know he was there. The handsome young face stood alone in the doorway and stared at her with silent intensity.

He wore a plain white T-shirt, dark charcoal gray jogging pants and black Timberland boots, but the way he looked at her was all it took. Gabriana almost immediately recognized who he was from around the way. The up close and personal encounter with Scholar took her by complete surprise, and although she had several reasons why she shouldn't, she still fell in love with him at first sight. It was nothing he said and it wasn't his game. It was simply him, and it's always been him.

Every since that night, they had been together every day. And since that togetherness began, all of her dreams were replaced with his.

As Gabriana lay on her bed, thinking about how much her life had changed, an idea hit her.

Gabriana knew what she could do. She had been at her mother's house for over two weeks and had not even thought to contact her girls. So far, every moment was spent with Mama, on the Internet, or talking on the phone with Toree. Gabriana spent so much time speaking with Toree because she wanted to keep tabs on Scholar. Since he had been on tour, they went from speaking three or four times a day to maybe twice at the most. Gabriana was trying to be understanding of his busy schedule, but her anxieties were running heavy. She missed her man. Removing her cell phone from the charger, she searched her contacts 'til she located Ciona's number. She pressed "Select" and waited for the connection. Ciona answered on the fourth ring.

"Hello?"

"Hi, baby girl," Gabriana said.

Pause

"The one and only Gabri, what's up?" Ciona responded dryly.

"Just wanted to see how you and Milan were doing. Let's get out tonight and get some dranks are something," Gabriana suggested.

"Nah, that's a'ight, chick. What's the real deal, your dude left the city without you and now you figure you got time for others?"

Pause

Clearly, Ciona had somewhat of an attitude. Gabriana played it cool though. "Look, girl, I miss y'all and you know how it is when you're in love. You spend every chance you can with your baby, right?"

Ciona was silent. Gabriana took a deep breath then playfully said, "Hellooo, Ci Ci, what's up girl? Don't be like that. Let's get Milan on the line and go somewhere, please."

Ciona broke the news. "Gabriana, I'm going to be real with you. Milan and myself feel like it's really messed up how you can't get a minute to even call and see how we are doing. We were your friends before Scholar was your man and you are a trip, girl. You know what though? That's all right, I don't want to go out and anyway, in case you haven't heard around the way, Milan just had a miscarriage and she's not feeling too good."

Gabriana was now the one quiet. Then she said , "Are you serious? How is she?"

"Gabriana, please. You would know if you really gave—"

"Ci, it's not like that, seriously. You're right. I should have been checking up," Gabriana cut in.

Ciona received another call trying to get through. "Hold on, Gabriana," she said before clicking over.

Almost immediately after being placed on hold, Gabriana's own line began to click with another caller. Glancing down at the caller ID on her new Sidekick, she saw that it was Scholar. "Dang," she said before clicking over.

Scholar was drunk and the first thing out of his mouth was, "Baby, I love you." This caught Gabriana off guard. It wasn't that he didn't tell her those words often, he just hadn't said them lately.

"Sweetie, I love you more. How is everything?" she asked, grabbing her stomach. After three years, Scholar still gave his girl butterflies.

"Gabri, straight up, I miss you and I am sending for you this weekend. Be ready to ride or die with your man." Gabriana smiled so hard her cheeks hurt.

"Scholar, oh, my God, are you serious? I'm ready, baby, whenever. I miss you so much."

Not even realizing it, Gabriana had gotten distracted that quick. She was so excited. She and Scholar talked for almost two hours and that was something they did not do once since his departure. After their conversation was over, Gabriana lay backward on her bed. She was smiling and beaming up at the ceiling, zoned, until she realized that she had left Ciona on the other end. "I'm tripping," she said, reaching over and grabbing her phone. Gabriana redialed Ciona's number, but there was no answer. She left a quick voicemail then searched for and retrieved Milan's number. The line rang and rang. No answer. Deciding against leaving a message for her friend, she hung up and tried again. There was still no answer. Gabriana hung up the line and sat the phone down next to her. "You know what? I'm going to head down to one of these little Monday night open mic sessions and get a drink." Gabriana was too excited about her upcoming reunion with Scholar to sit still.

When Gabriana entered the room, after showering, she glanced down at her phone still lying on the bed. There were three text messages pending. She opened the first two, which were divisions of one long message from Milan, and they read:

Gabriana, u kno what, you are whack, homie! Let me tell you why. First of all, you are as fake as a Barbie doll. Ask urself, who was down

41

with u b4 you got with Scholar? Second of all, I dn't kno abt Ciona but it hurts that u playd me 4 Scholar especially after I forgave yo fake az for stealing him in the first place. Dn't get it twisted tho, b'cuz like we discus'd when we talked abt it, me and him were never a couple and we never slept 2gther or none of tht but the point is, I confided in u when I told u how much I had a thing 4 him since my freshman yr when I transfer'd to his school. Still, what did u do? You slip'd behind my back and got up on him and I let it ride b'cuz we are women. But that's so grimy that you dn't come around anymore. You have no idea what I have been thru over the last few mths and I'm sure u don't care. So guess what...dn't call my phone anymore b'cuz it's FU2! – Milan.

Gabriana shot up from the bed. "This jealous, childish little girl," she gritted aloud. "Why is she sitting up tripping off *my* dude? Is she crazy? I'm about to let this cornball chick have it!" she exclaimed while rushing to put on her clothes. Gabriana intended to call Milan back as soon as she got out of Jannette's house. Lord knows her mama didn't need to hear the verbal assault that was about to go down on Milan. "Screw both of them lost chicks. I'm stepping out by myself. I don't need them."

Once she applied the last of her makeup, Gabriana grabbed her purse, threw on her coat and rushed out the door.

Inside the confinement of her car, Gabriana popped open her phone to call Milan back. That's when she realized she still had the second text pending. It was from Scholar. Excitedly, she pressed "Read."

~ 'Sup Kim, where u at? Meet me in 30 mins in rm 313. I'm thirsty 4u so dnt be taking 4ever! U need to bring all that wit u, nahmean :) ~ Scholar

Chapter 6

Gabriana drove in circles for another hour. It was after 12:00 am before she finally decided to go ahead into the open mic session at a little spot called Lights. After parking, she pulled down the overhead mirror and attempted to fix her makeup. Her eyes were swollen and red. "Whatever," Gabriana said and then exited the car. She had tried in vain to reach Scholar for the last hour, but he was "unavailable."

Inside the spot there was a nice semi-crowd. Gabriana went straight to the restroom. She was thankful that it was one of those unisex stalls that only serviced one at a time. She needed her privacy for a minute. Looking in the mirror, she said to herself, "Shake it off, girl, get it together." Unfortunately, her eyes showed what her heart really felt. Gabriana reached down into her huge Juicy Couture bag and retrieved the matching sunglasses. They were big and dark. Perfect. She applied enough gloss to her lips to take the attention away from any awkwardness her facial expression may have given off. With glasses on and a million thoughts on her mind, Gabriana exited the restroom and headed for the bar.

By her third glass of Remy Martin "straight up", Gabriana had gotten into the performances enough to temporarily remove the pain of Scholar's mistaken text. She signaled for the bartender and requested her fourth glass of the dark cognac. The guy standing next to her asked, "Can I ask why you are wearing shades inside? I mean, the lighting is already dim and all." He looked upward and circled his index finger for emphasis. Apparently, this guy found it a little comical, but Gabriana did not.

As nasty as she could muster it, Gabriana replied, "No, so shut the hell up, talking to me." She then gulped down her entire drink in one swig and paid the bartender after the fact. The guy simply walked off. About fifteen minutes or so later, the same dude was standing near the side of the stage, awaiting his introduction. Gabriana glared at him through her shades. Surprisingly, he looked back at her. She frowned up and returned her attention to the host.

"Ladies and gentlemen, some of y'all definitely know this guy right here, but for those of you who are new witnesses, I would like to introduce you all to Khali."

The audience cheered.

Khali stepped onto the stage with a cocky grin. He was of average height and weight. His face stood out with boyish round eyes. There was a genuine smoothness about him. His skin was an even brown, but there was a red glow to it. He wore a modest pair of True Religion jeans with white trimming, an all-white Polo hooded jacket and tan construction Timberland boots. His blue-and-white Yankees baseball cap faced forward, just above his long lashes. The guy possessed the most beautiful, thick eyelashes that Gabriana had ever witnessed on a man. Khali's only accessory was an all black face Kenneth Cole watch. There was no earring and no chain. No rings and no embezzled bracelets. Slightly tipsy, Gabriana said aloud to no one in particular, "He a'ight."

She thought he was kind of cute.

Khali looked toward the front audience, and then at the rude female who had all but spat on him in the back at the bar. He then began his words.

Who or what is a dreamer, sitting there disguising herself

Describing descriptions and feelings that she never really felt

Too unsure to understand His plans are always pure

She wants no part in using her gift, she wants a cure

As this stranger went on with his words, behind her shades, Gabriana opened the inside of her eyes. Unintentionally, she opened her mouth and moved her tongue. "What? How could he?" she asked, but without real words ever manifesting the questions verbally. Everything fell silent in her mind, and her ears refused to hear more. Then suddenly she regained alertness and captured the remaining words of Khali.

Nah, I'm not a psychic, a prophet, nor off my rocket

Just a cat that reads people like you, then builds his topic

And so it gets said just this once, I introduce

The proof, see Khali, another dreamer spit the truth

And then it was over.

Gabriana reached for her glass, but it was gone. The bartender had removed it as he wiped down the counter. It had been almost an hour since Khali left the stage and most of the audience had already cleared the venue. A lone bouncer walked the floor when the lights came on, but Gabriana still sat on the stool.

She had watched the stranger, "Khali," mingle for about thirty minutes after his performance. She watched him when he put his coat on and made his way out of the building. Never once, since the stage, did he look her way.

As nicely as he could, the bouncer approached Gabriana to inform her that the event was over and asked her to leave the premises. She returned to her car then opened her bag to retrieve her cell phone before starting the engine. Inside the purse, on top of all the clutter sat a plastic card. Despite whatever text the card was originally promoting, the bold permanent marker overrode it all. "Khali," she read aloud as she stared down at the name and number scribbled in huge font.

He had strategically dropped the card in her purse before he ever spoke to her.

Chapter 7

The weekend had finally arrived and Gabriana couldn't wait to board the flight westbound to L.A. She would soon be meeting up with Scholar. Since Monday night's omen via text, Gabriana remained quiet around the house. Jannette inquired about her status, but Gabriana gave her one look that told her mother to leave it alone. She never revealed the mistaken text message to Scholar. She didn't know if he ever realized it or not, but she never busted him out because she was not ready to deal with that side of the game. Gabriana had known Scholar to be many things, unpleasant at times, but she had never known him to be a cheater. She blocked the error from her mind and deleted the text right along with the memory of it. In her mind, there was no Kim or Nya. Scholar wouldn't play her like that. They were better than that. This Gabriana knew.

When the taxi arrived to shuttle Gabriana to the airport, she rolled her luggage into the living room where Jannette was seated in a chair asleep. "Mama, I'm leaving now," she whispered as she gently shook her mother. When Jannette opened her eyes, Gabriana froze for a moment. There were dark circles under her mother's eyes that stood out. Her mommy looked weary and a faint chill rushed through Gabriana's body. During her stay, she had noticed the strange differences in her mother's appearance, but naïve Gabriana would immediately shake it off in her mind. She was not ready to deal.

"Bye, sweetheart," her mother whispered back. Gabriana just stood there confused. This was not like Jannette. Her mother would always give her a hug and a lecture before allowing her to depart her presence for days. Something was definitely not right.

"Mommy, what's wrong?" she asked softly.

"Bye," was the only response Jannette offered before closing her eyes again. Gabriana kissed her mother's cheek and walked out the door.

~ ~ ~

L.A. was sweet. Scholar sent a limo to transport his girl back to a luxurious hotel suite he had reserved. When Gabriana slid the keycard into the electronic lock and entered the room, the first and only thing she saw was her dude, and only her dude. She didn't notice any of the gift bags he had laid out everywhere for her. She didn't even notice the twelve bottles of champagne, lining all four corners of the bed. Gabriana's sight was tuned on tunnel vision. All she saw was that face, at first. Then she looked him up and down.

Scholar was shirtless and seated on the edge of the bed. He was leaning forward, resting his elbows on his knees, doing nothing. It was like he was waiting for her. He wore army green, Sean Jean cargo shorts with chocolate-and-green military Nikes. A lone canary diamond earring stud set off the Breitling gold-and-yellow diamond watch he was sporting. The bright lights of that signature piece alone was enough to command the attention of the blind. Nothing else was needed on Scholar's body. Any other female, woman or girl, would have been too overwhelmed seeing such lavish jewels with their own eyes to not flip out. But Gabriana wasn't impressed by those material things as she took her man into full view. She was controlled by his presence alone. She still had not said a word, or caught her breath.

Scholar welcomed her in with a chuckle, then suddenly, he looked away. "Come here, Mama," he requested with diverted eyes.

Gabriana didn't budge. She was still involuntarily stuck in place. Scholar's bottom lip tucked beneath his bite before repeating, "I said come here. What are you waiting for?" This time he returned his gaze upon her. He smiled upward, then in one moment, Gabriana was setting up shop on Scholar's lap.

Her face nuzzled into his neck and inhaled his scent. *Sean Jean, I Am King.* Instinctively, Scholar placed his arm around her waist, but he kept his face forward. Gabriana stiffened her back, then slowly grabbed his face and turned it in the direction of her own. "Look at me. Scholar. Are you okay?"

Scholar briefly looked at Gabriana, then dropped his head.

He removed her from his lap and stood. With both hands, he reached for Gabriana's hands, pulling her up from the bed and into him. Gabriana missed him so much, in such a small amount of time. How could she bear ever being without him for longer? No chicks, no arguments, none of that meant anything. Scholar was a favored drug that Gabriana was passionately addicted to. She allowed him to hug her tightly around her waist as she tightened her own grip around his neck. For no less than a full minute, both Gabriana and Scholar held onto one another. Suddenly, nervous energy trickled through Gabriana's system. Without warning, her breath began to quicken. She tried to ease out of the hold, but Scholar wouldn't release her. Their eyes remained connected and the attention was strong. In fact, he pulled her in so close that there was no room to move around. Nothing else was optional to do, but kiss him. So that's what she did.

Gabriana kissed him like she was trying to paint a picture with her mouth. Before she could realize it, she had backed Scholar up against the wall. It seemed that her goal was to suck out every ounce of the personal air that belonged to his body. Gabriana wanted him to breathe *her.* He was hers, and this was *her* time.

She used the cunning art of a kiss to captivate him, and Scholar didn't resist.

Together, they remained in his suite for almost a full twenty-four hours. Everyone knew not to disturb them. Unless you were room service, you were not allowed to come anywhere near their personal space. This was *their* time.

The couple spent the entire weekend together. They partied hard with Scholar's entourage of friends. During the times they were alone, he took her shopping and wined and dined her at the finest beach-side resorts and city restaurants he could reserve. The final night of her L.A. visit, Gabriana and Scholar stayed up all night, joking around. They were up under each other until the crack of dawn. That morning, they decided to go out to the beach, just in time to watch the sunrise. Neither one of them spoke as they both watched God's new mercy spread over the sky. Gabriana sat still with her back facing Scholar. The scene reminded her of a dream she had years ago when she was teenager. In the dream, the sky was the same color orange as the color above her now, except the sun was missing. Below the sky there was a great shadow cast all about the land. Gabriana never understood that dream, but she never forgot it. She remembered asking God what it meant, and the only explanation that would come to mind was the thought of the Lord being absent. Contemplating her memories, and also thinking about another dream she had the night before, Gabriana wanted desperately to discuss her real thoughts and dreams with Scholar, but she was afraid. Scholar never liked her dreams and the last time she'd made the attempt, he had threatened to leave her. Nope, there was no way she would make that mistake again. Scholar intercepted her thoughts, reached behind Gabriana and pulled her to him. He held her tight. In fact, she couldn't remember him holding her so tight before. Gabriana closed her eyes and embraced the strong biceps that held her. There was so much she wanted to say. Not knowing where to start, she asked Scholar, "Why weren't you named after your father? Why did Lil' Cobi get the name instead of you?"

She had always wondered about that, but knowing how sensitive he could be about his father, she never asked until now. "Because he told my mother that he wanted me to be my own man." Surprising Gabriana, he offered more details. "He started calling me Scholar when I was like nine years old because he wanted me to get my own knowledge out here. To this day, I think that's why it's so hard for anybody to tell me anything," he laughed. "I remember my little friends used to tease me, saying, *Nigga, you ain't smart enough to carry that name.*"

Gabriana interrupted. "You are smart. You're not only smart enough to carry that name, but you're smart enough to carry everybody else associated with that *name*, period."

Scholar was silent for a moment, then concluded his thoughts. "Even though that's what my father wants from me, I still find myself feeling like I'm riding his coattails and that bothers me. Straight up. That's why I'm out here sacrificing so hard. I have to go extra hard for my own respect, fo'real. That's all I want, is the respect out here."

Once again, silence reclaimed the beach. There were so many more questions that she wanted to ask this man, but she didn't. Gabriana wanted to know about every thought going through his head, but she never asked any more questions that morning. He had just proven to her at that moment that he was open to answer her questions with honesty. Regardless, she still hesitated. She left the unchartered territories of the man she loved to ponder alone within his head. Gabriana was unaware that Scholar wanted to ask her many questions as well. Although her dreams scared him, he was still curious about them. He was curious about her. Scholar had never admitted it, but he was also curious about Jannette, and her perception of God. *Why is she so passionate about her beliefs? What makes that woman so confident that she is right?* he would ask himself every time he saw her from a distance. His own mother never talked much about God. The little that he did know, he had learned from an incarcerated father.

51

~~~

Mama...who exactly is God?

God is the almighty Creator that rules over everything...now give me a moment, I'm on the phone.

So what does God look like?

Keon, you see me on the phone! Please, baby, go ask your daddy. He thinks he knows it all, anyway.

During his early years, Scholar was very close with his mother, Tina. Out in the streets, she was a very hard woman, but in the confines of her own home, she was easygoing with her children, especially Scholar. When she wasn't out in the streets, making moves for Jacobi Sr., it was all about Toree and Scholar, but mostly Scholar. The two children were only one year apart in age, but their personalities were like night and day. It seemed that Tina would always concern herself with her son more often than her elder daughter. He was the apple of her eye, her prized possession. Tina saw something in her son; therefore, she always showered him with extra affection. He was her blessed child. Keon Jacob Jamison, also known as "Scholar," was officially her favorite.

Jacobi Sr. completely despised the misunderstood relationship that his wife shared with their son. In his opinion, it was disgusting. He believed that no male child should cling to his mother, period. To him, that type of bond was unnatural and couldn't be healthy for the boy's development and behavior. Here and there, he would argue his point saying, "Keon is not a daughter...he is a SON! He should only be bonding with his father in ALL ways, with ME! Not YOU. Spend that time with Toree, she's the one who needs you."

Tina knew Jacobi was right about Toree, but still, there had to be a hint of crazy in him for sure if he thought that she was going to let up on Scholar. There were quite a few times when Jacobi had the audacity to threaten to replace Tina as Scholar's mother if she didn't fall back more. After that threat started coming up, she knew that her husband was nuts. Still, Tina continued to relate to her children the way that she wanted to. There was no doubt that she respected her husband's gangsta persona on so many other levels, but that was out in the other world. She didn't comply with him at all when it came to her babies. Or her baby, Scholar—she chose that battle with honor.

As Scholar began his adolescence, that's when Jacobi Sr. really began to lose all patience for him leaning on his mother so much. He started displaying his disapproval of the relationship more and more, until it became a very serious issue within their home. Although, Scholar and Toree never disclosed their family problems outside of the house walls, there were many arguments that grew into physical fights between their parents that should have been reported. There were various accounts where the disagreeing exchanges went from verbal fire to violence. This tore Scholar apart because much of the time, he was the topic of the altercations. Toree often had an attitude with him because she wasn't blind or deaf. She knew a huge chunk of their woes were a result of her brother.

Ultimately, one of those innumerable fights ended up changing all of their lives forever.

That particular evening, Jacobi crept into the house. Before anyone could notice his arrival, he'd overheard a conversation between Scholar and Tina that sparked all hell and fury within him.

"Keon, I don't want anymore detention notifications from your school. This is the sixth notice. What is going on with you?"

Scholar was very honest with her. "This girl," he mumbled.

"What do you mean *this girl*? What are you talking about?"

"There's this girl who doesn't pay me any attention and…"

Fourteen-year-old Scholar went on to confess his crush for a girl in his classroom who never paid him any attention when he would try and talk to her. He admitted that he did little extra things in class to get her attention. He even wrote raps about her and would perform them out loud for the other students to hear. But really, it was all for the girl's ears. He really wanted her to be impressed, but the more she ignored him, the harder he felt he had to try. This was the reason he stayed in trouble. He was receiving the wrong attention, from the wrong person—the teacher.

Tina knew Scholar wasn't a bad kid. She understood him and talked openly to her child. Jacobi listened intensively as his wife counseled Scholar on love and better ways for getting a girl to notice him. She was not just telling him things as a mother, but also schooling him from a woman's perspective.

"Keon, the female species is very complex. If you're really into one of us, you have to pursue us and that's where the challenge comes in. You have to weigh your options and just…" Tina paused for a second. "If you truly feel she's worth it, just try other approaches. More creative ones."

"Yeah, I know. That's why I write the raps. That's my way of—"

Scholar was speaking honestly with his mother when Jacobi crashed through the partially closed door. He looked so angry that his mouth appeared distorted when it moved. Foamy spittle sprayed a mist when Jacobi began barking. He looked right at Tina and said, "Get out. Get out of my house, now!"

Scholar and Tina were both shocked by the crazed looking man before them, so they just sat there. Tina quickly gathered her words and tried to protest, but Jacobi had already snatched her up and tossed her out the bedroom door like she was a doll. She tried to recover and bounce back into the room, but Jacobi grabbed her, and threw her body completely down to the floor. He then turned his wrath to Scholar.

"You are soft! You are fourteen years old…fourteen, nigga! You mean to tell me that you can't control your emotions good enough to handle your business? What does that say about you? You have to show yourself off as a clown in order to gain attention? What did I teach you? You know how I feel about you educating yourself. What you are showing people is that you are not smart. You need to focus!"

Jacobi's words struck Scholar with the impact of a physical strike. He listened in embarrassment and disbelief while Jacobi Sr. continued to scream at him.

"I ain't raising no corny nigga. Stand up!"

Scholar stood immediately. He looked straight into the eyes that were looking straight into him. He knew about his father's incorrigible reputation out in the streets, so Scholar hated when his old dude was disappointed in him over anything.

"I'm ashamed of you right now. I don't respect you, and I won't respect you 'til you learn to earn it! Get your mind right. If you don't learn to straighten up and focus, you are going to have a very short life. People use and kill people they don't respect. You're worried about love and crushing when you should concern yourself with getting your respect up. Hoes and all the extra perks come after the fact. Get your respect up, little nigga! It all starts there and that starts now because later is too late."

Tina continued to yell things out in the background, but Scholar couldn't hear her. All he could take in were the hurtful words of his father as they came his way.

55

"You're at school, missing out on learning all because of your feelings for some girl who don't even like you. Are you that simple? Man-up
and smarten-up. Be about your business, always!"

BOOM

Jacobi delivered the forceful blow to Scholar's frail chest as if he
were striking a grown man. Scholar flew backward into the wall. Before
he could fully realize that his wind was knocked out, he was hit again by
the same iron fist.

BOOM

That's when Tina physically jumped in it. No one was going to abuse
her child. Those punches sounded too brutal to not be disturbing to any
mother. She clawed and scratched, and did everything she could to keep
Jacobi from hitting her son again. By the end of the fight, she and a wad
of her clothes and belongings were thrown out onto the front yard. As
much as she screamed and yelled out there, Tina was not allowed back
into the house, and that's how it remained for weeks.

Eventually, Tina was unable to stand being away from her children,
so she went and did what she felt she had to do in order to regain some
control.

After numerous failed attempts at convincing Jacobi Sr. to let her
return home, Tina concluded what had to be done, so that's what she did.
In order to get rid of the opposing force, she snitched her own husband
out to the police. Without any shame, whatsoever, she dropped a dime on
Jacobi Sr. All was fair in love and war.

It was early in the morning when Jacobi was placed under arrest in
front of his son and daughter. They both watched from the front porch in
horror as their father was led through the yard toward one of what looked

like an entire county of cop cars. The red-and-blue flashing lights made the scene look like Christmas time. A modest unit of SWAT team officials roamed in and out of the house. Their presence alone commanded the full attention of the entire block, but Scholar couldn't take his eyes off his father. Initially, the police told Jacobi Sr. that they were taking him away for questioning on a murder, but that was also before they brought all kinds of weapons out of their house. Scholar knew he would never see his father at their home again. He just felt it inside, and as his eyes were beginning to swell up, his father looked directly at him. The detective was motioning for Jacobi to get inside the car, but instead, he froze in place and stared right at his only son. "Focus," he said. "Stay out of your feelings and focus, or you will lose everything, sooner than later. This is a cold world."

That was all Jacobi Sr. had to say, and that was more than what was needed. Instantly, those words spawned a sea of seeds within Scholar, including one of fear. After Jacobi was locked down for over a month, Scholar would awake in the middle of the night and destroy his room. He would be sound asleep then suddenly, out of the blue, he would wake up and trash everything he could get his hands on. Tina tried various methods to calm her son down during the outbursts, but nothing helped. The routine was very troublesome for the newly single mother. When Tina couldn't take it anymore, she became a clone of Jacobi Sr.

One night, Scholar arose and went into his rampage, but that was to become the final night. Tina was fed up and she snapped.

She burst into Scholar's room with the rage of a bull. She grabbed a dresser drawer from out of its shelf and slung it through the wall. Then she grabbed another one and swung it at her son, over and over, until he was backed into a corner. That's when she went in.

"Whatever nightmares you are having cannot be worse than mine. Tonight it's over. I don't ever want to see you react to another emotion. You need to be a man. Man up! I am pregnant, do you hear me? Preg-nant and I don't need this from you!" Tina screamed her confession through anger.

"I'm having a baby, Keon! And your father is GONE, and he's never coming home, so I need you to become whatever it is that you are to become. Take the respect that your father has left out here as an inheri-tance and man up! Stop all these tantrums, and hold all those weak, corny emotions in. MAN UP!"

For Scholar, that was a revelation that he never shared with anyone. That moment was one of transformation and metamorphosis. Jacobi Sr. did get a chance to come home a year later, but two years later, he was placed back in prison—for good. That realization, along with the crown that his parents trained his head for, left Scholar with no choice. He had to man up. Both Tina and Jacobi Sr. had scorned their son into posi-tion by way of words alone. Jacobi Sr. left one strict order with Scholar the day he was sentenced to life and that was to take care of home, and *survive.*

From that day on, Tina stayed on Scholar's back about everything. In a way, Scholar felt betrayed by his mother. She had never in his life been that harsh with him, but most of all, she had never displayed any raw *streetness* toward her children until that point in her life. As far as Scholar could remember, his mother was not that woman. But now she was, and that left him feeling alone, because to him, she was also a friend. Now he didn't really trust her, the same way he didn't completely trust his father. They were like one being. Both were street people, and at the end of the day, Tina was a boss lady. After her husband was sentenced to a life sentence, she became her real self, full-time, and that included in front of her children. She had to survive, and she needed them to survive.

Hustlers, gangsters, whatever you want to call them, Scholar's parents

58

were amongst the same characteristics of people that Jacobi Sr. had warned him plenty of times not to put too much faith into.

Anyone and everyone will let you down. Even the people closest to you. In a way, everyone is about themselves, so be about yourself. You are the ruler of your own universe, not anyone else's.

Despite his own actions, or even his father's, Scholar still felt that his mother had really crossed the line when she let him down. But it wasn't just her. His father disappointed him too. He respected their gangsta ways, but he didn't respect them. Just like he felt they didn't respect him. It was a lot to hold all inside, but also too deep to explain to people, so he managed to keep it to himself.

It was during that time in his life when he, himself, had completely changed over. Stemming from the very first time that Tina had flipped on him, Scholar no longer had any nightmares. At least not that anyone knew about. When Scholar began to teach himself how to suppress his emotions, the nose bleeds started, and with the nose bleeds came the sharp cramps.

There was not one person on planet earth who knew about those bloody moments or even the severe stomachaches that Scholar's anxiety attacks brought on because he hid them well. He never let anyone know about any of that. Those were his secrets and he knew no help, so he sought none. He kept many secrets from everyone—even Gabriana. "No one needs to know everything," he told himself. *"I'm positive she doesn't tell me everything, herself!"*

Scholar looked out into the mass of waves. When he felt his mind begin to click around too fast, he released a silent, but strong, exhale. Gabriana leaned back closer. She could feel the change in the rise and fall of his chest cavity. Slowly, but firmly, she squeezed his hands. It was a small way of reassuring Scholar that she was there with him, and that calmed him. Gabriana didn't know what was going through his being at the time, but she could definitely feel something radiating. She just didn't know what. Gabriana hesitated when it came to digging deeper into Scholar's world for some strange reason.

He kissed Gabriana gently on her neck as he continued to think. Lately, Scholar had been wondering how similar Jannette and Gabriana actually were. He wondered if one day, she, too, would follow Jannette's *God* and leave him behind. If she did, he wondered if she would come back and keep it real with him. Would and could she help him to understand things?

There was an invisible wall that separated their understanding of each other and the world around them. Gabriana wanted to tear down that wall, she just wasn't sure how and if the feeling was mutual.

If only she knew the truth to that matter.

~~~

The final leg of the tour took the crew through many different cities and towns. After the tour, Scholar had to settle down in Miami for two additional months while the label and his management were preparing for his debut album's release. There were still more songs and collaborations that needed to be recorded. There were also videos and appearances that needed to be filmed. While unpacking their luggage in yet another hotel room, Scholar smiled over at Gabriana with that smile she loved so much on him.

"What are you smiling about," she asked, returning a smile. Scholar just laughed and asked Gabriana if she was ready to return back home. Her reply was a simple one, but it came rapid, "No. For what?"

Gabriana walked over to Scholar and playfully shoved him in his chest. "Don't tell me you're tired of me, nigga. What, you hinting around or something?" Gabriana was about to push Scholar again, but he grabbed both of her hands. Gabriana giggled and tried to pull free. Scholar squeezed down tighter and looked into her face until her smile dissipated. His voice took on a more somber tone as he said, "I'm serious. So you just want to hang around me? There's nothing else you would rather be doing back at home?"

Gabriana tried to force her hands from his grip. This time Scholar opened his hands and freed her. Gabriana folded her arms across her chest and briefly frowned, then smirked. "Don't get it twisted for a second. I have no life there without you...*you* are my life," she said, slowly wrapping her arms around his neck. "You are the only thing I'm living for."

Together, they both laughed at that one.

And so did God.

With the exception of the wild clubs and parties the promoters had her man attending, to Gabriana, everything was just perfect. She and Scholar were getting along well. She stuck so close by his side that the groupie chicks didn't have a chance. Whenever the shows were over, so were their fantasies because Gabriana was not having it. She could not believe the extent that some of those star-struck females would go through to get backstage. She would watch in utter disbelief at the acts of lust and stupidity that would go on between these women and the males within their entourage. On many occasions, Gabriana would have to boldly make her presence known in order to banish any glimmers of hope those females may have had about getting with Scholar. Although she displayed a confident stance, the competition was slowly biting away at her nerves. It was vastly becoming too much.

One restless night, while lying in bed with Scholar, Gabriana thought

61

about the conversation that she and Scholar had before he went to sleep.

Lying on top of Scholar, Gabriana had jokingly asked him, "Baby, what do you think about marriage?"

Scholar squinted his eyes, but said nothing. "Oh, so you're not going to answer me," she asked with a frown.

"I'm *not* thinking about it," Scholar said, moving her off of him.

This confused Gabriana. Just moments before, he had been so affectionate. He had told her so many times that night how much he loved her. Within an instant, his demeanor had flipped. A shocked Gabriana just looked at Scholar. There was hurt in her eyes, but she tried to play her feelings off.

"Yeah, I know, but...you know how much I love you, Scholar. You just got through telling me how much you love me, too. You just said that there's nothing you wouldn't do for me." she reminded him.

"What? Girl, come on, that was in the heat of the moment," Scholar replied with an agitated look on his face.

Gabriana's eyes immediately watered. She wanted to speak, but the words got caught in her throat. Scholar just shook his head and looked away.

Inside of his heart, Scholar felt that he did love Gabriana. Sometimes he would just say cruel things to her just to keep her quiet. He mostly did this whenever she struck a nerve. In truth, he actually had thought about making Gabriana his wife, but he had trust issues.

The atmosphere became muted, and apprehension lingered. Scholar tilted his head to the side and looked over at Gabriana. "Look, I'm sorry. I didn't mean for that to come out like that," he apologized with sincerity.

Gabriana ran her hands through her hair then sternly said, "Don't ever front on me like that...ever again. You know just like I do, you're always saying you love me. The real question is... do you love me enough to wife me?"

Scholar turned his head toward the wall opposite of where Gabriana lay next to him. Becoming frustrated, Gabriana grabbed his chin and repositioned his face toward her own.

"Scholar, I'm asking you—"

Scholar cut her off saying, "Yes! I mean, yeah, I definitely love you, but I just don't know about marriage yet, Gabriana. Right now, I'm just happy that you are my girl. Leave it at that."

Silence

"Nah, Scholar. That's not good enough for me," Gabriana rebutted, then paused. "I want to be wifey."

For a moment, Scholar appeared as if he were dazed by her words. He then removed himself from the bed and walked into the bathroom, closing the door behind him. Gabriana could hear him relieving himself, then the faucet water ran. She never once took her eyes off the bathroom door. A short moment later, he resurfaced and returned next to her side of the bed.

Lying on his back, Scholar bit down on his bottom lip and looked into her eyes. "You really love me, huh?"

Gabriana's heart skipped a beat before she gently answered. "Do you mean to tell me that you have not noticed? I love you *very* much. Some-times, I feel like I love you more than myself. It's you who comes first."

Seconds passed before anyone spoke. Then in a serious tone, Scholar asked, "So you're saying that you'll never cheat on me or leave me, right? Not for nothing or nobody?"

Gabriana leaned over and kissed his nose. She then replied, "Never, baby."

"Never," he mocked.

"Never," she repeated through a slight grin. She then lifted his left hand to her lips and placed a soft kiss on the back. The gesture indicated her respect for his position, and how she bowed down to it. There was no shame.

Scholar responded with eyes that spoke a million unspoken words. The two of them just lay there in their own thoughts until Scholar fell asleep. Now alone with her thoughts, Gabriana promised to a sleeping Scholar, "Even if you never marry me, I will never break my commitment to you, baby. Never."

Precisely at the same moment, Gabriana's cell phone began to buzz. She continued to lay there. At first she thought that maybe it was Khali.

Despite her love for Scholar, Gabriana had been secretly emailing and talking to her new friend every lone chance she got. He intrigued her and challenged her mentally. Although she had no intention of hurting Scholar in any way, she had unconsciously opened up a door.

The buzzing stopped. Then the buzzing started again.

Nah, dude wouldn't blow me up like that. He's way too cool for that nonsense. Not wanting to awake Scholar, she slowly removed herself from the bed and picked up the phone. The word *Private* glowed across the screen. Gabriana hesitated answering the call, but the buzzing continued. Stepping into the bathroom and closing the door, she connected the call.

"Who is this and what do you want?"

The older woman's voice on the other end asked, "Gabriana?"

At this point, her heartbeat had now begun to accelerate. The woman should be in bed at this time, no matter what time zone she resided in. "Yes," was all Gabriana replied.

Less than a minute later, Gabriana's phone was on the bathroom floor and she was screaming and shaking Scholar awake. "Oh, my God, Scholar, get up now!"

Scholar sent her home on the next thing flying. When she boarded that plane, Gabriana could have never imaged how much things would never be same.

Chapter 8

Two long months had passed since Gabriana's return to St. Louis. Jannette had been released only three days after being hospitalized for what she told her daughter was an enlarged heart condition. Satisfied with her mother's stabilization, Gabriana anticipated returning to Miami to be with Scholar. When she made the contact to inform him of this, he suggested that she remain with her mother for the remainder of the month. Two months later, Scholar still would not permit Gabriana to return to his side. The excuse he gave her was that the time was not right, and his hectic schedule would not allow him enough space to properly attend to her needs. Things were becoming complicated between them. Gabriana started out patient with the situation, but as the weeks went on she had become enraged. On too many occasions, she would contact Scholar and hear all sorts of females in the background. Remembering the vulgar activities she had witnessed from the tour, she would snap out and express her frustrations by yelling at the top of her lungs through his phone.

"What is going on?! Do you think I'm stupid?! Who are all those females I'm always hearing in the background?!"

Sometimes she would even cry, which was out of her character. "I need to come out there immediately, stop playing me! Please, I can't take being away from you for another day. Is it another woman? Please tell me if you are cheating on me because I'm not understanding why I can't come and be with you."

Scholar would only enhance her anger and suspicions. He would say things like, "Gabriana, fo'real, don't keep blowing up my phone. You know what I do, so stop tripping. I'm tired of going through this with you." Lately, he had been reversing the game and manipulating Gabriana. Threatening her position, he would say things like, "Gabriana, do you want me to leave you alone completely?" He would even scream at her, telling her harshly, "I am on my video set! You are going to hear females because they are vixens and they're supposed to be here! What do you expect? You're real dumb right now…stay off my phone with all that crying! I don't want to hear it," then hang up on her. You would have thought he was talking to a child. Scholar came off completely insensitive to the fact that this was the first time that he and Gabriana had spent that much time apart since they'd met. The separation may have been somewhat welcomed by him, but to his girlfriend it was very hard to get used to.

After many useless tears, eventually, Gabriana began to accept her powerless circumstances. With her girls, Ciona and Milan still not talking to her, she began to spend a lot of her time with Khali. They would do simple things around the way, although this dude was far from simple.

Khali would take Gabriana to places like urban art shows. He would even draw pictures for her then explain the inspiration behind them. Sometimes he would drive her outside of the city to find hidden lakes and watch the stars, or just lay back in the openness of nature. This helped her to relax and relieve stress. Although she enjoyed their little ventures, it was Khali's conversation that wheeled her in. She felt so comfortable around him. She could talk to him for hours on hours and not grow tired of his voice. His perspective on life captured her attention, and her starved curiosity kept her wanting more.

One night, while lounging in a hotel room with Khali, Gabriana found herself really studying him. She was beginning to really *like* him. Sparking up her freshly rolled blunt, she leaned back up against the pillows of the large bed and watched Khali sit at the oak desk and write in his book.

"What are you always writing in that book?" she asked him with a smirk.

There was a brief delay before Khali answered. "Why, Gabriana? You know you're not really interested in what I'm over here writing." Gabriana didn't respond. She just continued to hit her blunt and stare at him.

Khali looked up at her, then went on to say, "You know the only thing, or should I say the only person that you are concerned with fo'real is that nigga Scholar." He was taunting her, but only doing so at that moment because she had just ended a phone conversation with Scholar in his presence. Khali secretly despised when she ignored him to talk to *that nigga*.

"So what, you hating on my man?"

"Never," he answered with a scowl. "But I'm not feeling nothing about that dude on no levels, you hear me?"

"Why? What exactly aren't you 'feeling' about him? What is your problem?"

"I just don't like him. I don't have a problem with him—yet."

"Yet? So what is that suppose to mean?" Gabriana demanded to know.

Khali shook his head in disgust, then shot back, "Yet! What, you don't know what that word means or something?"

"Khali, I don't get you. Don't get smart. You're always—"

"Let me tell you something, a'ight." Khali stood from his seat to look squarely at Gabriana. "Don't ever put that man on my path. That's what I mean. Don't ever put him in position to have to come at me the wrong way. I work with a short fuse when it comes to niggas like that. Believe that. I'm not the guy for unaware niggas to ever play with, or come at in any type of threatening way. I don't take well to that at all. I'm just warning you. Scholar don't—"

"Look, fall back with all of that," Gabriana retorted. She was getting more agitated by the second. "My man knows nothing about you. And anyway, he may be messed up in a lot of ways, but he got talent, and he's getting crazy paid right now. You don't even know him so don't go all off into what type of nigga you think he is, cuz you don't know."

Khali was well-aware of who the nigga Scholar was. Scholar had went on to release an early debut album last month and was the talk of the town because of the numbers he ran his first week of sales. Scholar had broke all types of records, and the record label executives were proud of their wise decision to push their artist out sooner than later. Scholar's buzz was like wildfire, or a phenomenon. Nothing they had ever seen happen so quickly. He took the world by storm and everyone was talking. Still, Khali didn't like the dude one bit. He saw straight through him and was not impressed.

"Man, fu—" He caught himself. "Anyway, I'm not impressed with your boy, so you can save the sale's pitch for somebody else."

After a couple seconds of silence, he continued his rant. "Real talk, there ain't no hate, it's just that I deal with a whole other kind of people, and I carry a whole 'nother way of thinking on my shoulders, and I got bigger burdens," Khali confessed.

"And what exactly would they be?" Gabriana asked with a hint of sarcasm. She already knew the distinction between the two men, she just wanted to press Khali's buttons. She was successful in her attempt.

"Well, first of all, I'm a thirty-one-year-old grown *man* and I know how to treat women," he struck back, hitting Gabriana below the belt.

Embarrassed, she glanced down at the bed and remained silent.

Khali continued, "You float around town like you're the queen bee," He said aggressively. "Inside, you know what really goes on. It's not a secret and everybody knows the deal, Gabriana. Obviously, everyone except for you. This nigga be on all kinds of DVDs and media sites, chilling with all types of chicks. And where are you during all of this? He's super hyped up, talking about niggas in these other cities, and on these other labels like they won't see him or something. This clown ain't been in the game a year and he got real hate surrounding him, niggas wanna see him *already*! That ain't good. But you're the *proud* woman." Khali waved her off with his hand.

Gabriana's eyes glossed over with anger.

"You can't be serious. What? You think that nigga love you?" Khali laughed. Because if you do then you don't know what love is. And if he thinks he loves you, then he got issues with the knowledge, too!"

Gabriana said nothing.

"Yeah, that's what I thought. You should try a real man one day," he added.

"And who would that be, you?" she shot back.

Khali took a deep breath then licked his lips. "Gabriana, look, we hang out and all, but you don't know much about me. I don't know who or what you take me for, but you got a lot to learn, love."

Khali walked over to Gabriana and removed the blunt from her fingers. Taking up a seat on the bed in front of her, he began toking the weed.

"Man, whatever," was all Gabriana finally replied. She looked everywhere in the room, except in front of her where Khali sat, looking at her.

Khali knew he had just gone hard on Gabriana, but he didn't care. He always gave her straight talk from day one of their friendship. But Gabriana showed very little appreciation for that. In a way, she felt that Khali took life too seriously, but at the same time, she highly admired and respected him for that very thing. There was something about the "Khali" guy that just pulled at Gabriana. He definitely shot arrows at her soul, but Gabriana took his admiration for granted. She never really asked him too much about himself. She only accepted what he offered. She knew that he had lived the majority of his life on the east coast, spreading between states over there, but she never inquired deeper. There were many times when Khali would call Gabriana up with conversation for her, but she would be preoccupied. A lot of those times she would be laughing, smoking and joking around with Toree, or whoever else was in her background, only giving Khali part of her attention. He recognized this, and he wasn't stupid, but still he was there, ready to be of assistance whenever she felt stressed or lonely. Whenever they would link up in person, their time together was blissful, and Gabriana consistently, and mindlessly flirted with him. Khali had no complaints about that 'cause he did the same thing to her. He was definitely digging Gabriana. It was only whenever Scholar was on her phone, or when she was in the presence of his family, that she revealed a part of herself that turned Khali off.

"You don't understand," Gabriana mumbled.

"No, don't put that off on me. It's *you* who don't understand," Khali said pointing a finger at her. His tone was now softer. "Let me tell you something, Gabriana. That book over there, the one you always see me writing in, that's my book of rhymes, my book of poetry and my book

72

of dreams. I know who you are, you just don't fully know who *I* am. Word?"

Gabriana looked up at Khali. He had her attention, just as he had the first night they had met. Although she never brought up that poem, or whatever it was to him, sometimes at night she would remember it, and wonder where it came from and why.

"This is a real, real world out here," Khali stressed. "Everything I say, everything I do, everything I write, everything I think about and everything around my existence is REAL to me. Life is more than money and fame, or chickens to me. Things run so deep out here, there's a whole other side of things that people don't or won't acknowledge. It's like their minds won't allow their brains to process it all, so they play in shallow waters." Khali passed the blunt back to Gabriana and continued. "When I was like four years old, my granddaddy took me and taught me how to swim. He didn't take me to the kiddies' pool down the street either. He took me all the way to the ocean and taught me. Yeah, real talk. Although I didn't at the time, now I understand perfectly well why he did that. He was planting a seed within me. He taught me to learn to do even the simplest of things on a deeper level."

Gabriana dropped the roach into the ashtray and placed it on the side of the bed. As Khali sat in front of her with his legs stretched, Gabriana leaned over and placed her head in his lap. She didn't say anything. She just closed her eyes and listened.

"Gabriana, don't let these niggas out here sell you dreams and feed you lies. Don't let them tell you deep things, then only show up with paper-thin actions. It shouldn't work like that. Hold niggas accountable. Don't hand out your soul, make a nigga earn your heart. I don't care how much loot they have. At the end of the day, if you ain't officially the wife, then none of the riches is yours anyway. The only thing you will eventually end up owning is heartache, Ma. Know that."

Chapter 9

The little girl sat on her mother's lap, trembling. The tears wouldn't stop falling. "Bri-Bri, baby, listen to me, there's no one in that bathroom," her mother said. The little girl cried even harder saying, "Yes, yes there is...she tried to grab me!" The mother removed the child from her lap and began walking her toward the bathroom. The little girl began to scream louder and tried to stop walking. Her mother began dragging her up the stairs and toward the open door, leading into the dark bathroom. "No, no, please I can't go in there." As the mother pulled her daughter into the bathroom the little girl closed her eyes. Her mother then released her hand. "Mommy, please. Noooo!" Suddenly, she didn't hear anything. "Mommy," she cried. There was still no answer. When the child opened her eyes...

Gabriana awoke. She looked around the dark room, then rubbed the muscular arm that was wrapped tightly around her. "Scholar," she whispered. Slightly turning her head toward his, she saw Khali sleeping. That's when the state of their being together hit her.

What did I do?

Gabriana lay there in confusion about what had taken place a couple hours earlier. When she slid her hand under the sheets and across her own body, it became painfully obvious. She immediately cursed herself. She knew exactly what had taken place. This was the second time, since she had been back in town, that they had made that same mistake.

For over two months since her return, there had been way too many nights that she and Khali spent together in different hotel rooms. That was inappropriate in itself, but still, Gabriana justified it. She didn't have her own place, and she didn't always want to be at Jannette's, so she would lounge in hotels. Not wanting to be alone the majority of the time, Gabriana would invite Khali to spend the night with her. The energy when they were alone would sometimes get very intense, but still, for the first month everything remained innocent. That was, until they slipped up the first time.

Gabriana felt horrible about cheating on Scholar, but he had her so down during that time that she was ultimately prone to make that error. She knew it was wrong. What she and Khali did, and how they did it, caused a prolonged minute for Gabriana to forgive herself. However, she never eased up on hanging out with Khali. She figured that they could just restore their platonic friendship and move on. But that wasn't the case. She was falling for him, and so, she ended up sleeping with him again.

Earlier, while lying across Khali's lap, Gabriana had allowed herself to drift into a state of semi-unconsciousness.

Maybe he's the one...maybe? The question tumbled around her mind.

Lying there, Gabriana had slipped into another zone. It was a comforting place where her thoughts were filled with every word Khali had been feeding her lately. She ran them all over her brain and spirit. Inside of his floating words, for the first time, she thought she truly saw him for who he was. She then found herself wondering why he came into her life.

She thought about their first time together. Both she and Khali had tried to make light of the encounter by calling it the "big payback." Even though, she cried about it to Khali until they were able to laugh about it together, Gabriana knew that they were really just lying to themselves. All the joking about that passionate mistake was just a mechanism to mask the confusion that they really felt for each other.

Gabriana's soul was faded by her thoughts until Khali brought her back into the physical realm.

His touch was smooth, but manly. She hadn't twitched a muscle when his hand danced in slow motion underneath her shirt, then all across her back. What kicked off as gentle kneads soon progressed into a sensual massage. Gabriana took in the feeling until she couldn't take it anymore. She sat up to looked at Khali. She wanted to see exactly what she saw and that was everything she needed at the moment.

So she touched his face.

When he allowed her to feel his skin Gabriana arose from her position, so she could straddle him.

Khali released a sharp breath and shook his head disapprovingly when Gabriana wrapped her arms around him. She needed to feel secure, but mostly, she needed his energy. She pushed the baseball cap from his head. When she tried to remove his shirt, the look in his eyes said it all.

Khali pushed her arms and hands away. "Don't, you know how you felt about the first time."

Gabriana simply replaced her arms around him with ease and strength. "I want to," she pronounced in a whisper. She wanted to ensure him that she knew exactly what she was doing.

"Nah. No. Not if you're gonna be thinking about that nigga, and having regrets. I'm not the one for you to play games with *all* the time. I'm not your rebound nigga. Chill 'cause…"

Gabriana silenced him with a kiss. She leaned her forehead onto his. She continued to peck his lips and face until their aggression picked up considerably. This time she removed his shirt successfully.

As they kissed, the movements felt different. It felt like artwork. Gabriana couldn't pinpoint the exact feeling, but she knew it felt strange, and at the same time, she liked it. She felt his admiration for her entirely. So entirely, she wanted him to feel hers—completely—with no Scholar on her mind. Her body and thoughts, if but for a short, stolen moment, were strictly for him. Whatever Khali wanted was his for taking. Gabriana was ready and willing to let him know it.

From there, there wasn't anything or anyone that could stop what was happening. Everything seemed to take a life of its own, and the inevitable had taken place inside that hotel room, once again.

There was no turning back from what had been done. There was no undoing it, and with that fact to deal with, Gabriana began to silently cry as she dug her nails into the bed. It was over with, but the guilt was very real and tormenting. Khali had warned her, but she didn't listen. Now, she was feeling it—again.

Scholar...I need to call Scholar.

Khali was holding onto Gabriana for dear life. But she needed to get to her phone, so she needed to get up. Gabriana slowly pulled the sheets down. When she tried to remove her body, Khali clutched her tighter.

"No. Please, just chill," he uttered to her from behind. His breath was warm on her skin, and with his kisses on the back of her neck, the situation was escalading beyond overwhelming. It was becoming painful. The feeling was detrimental. Gabriana reached forward and dug her nails into the bed again. She was confused, and couldn't express it in any other way except to squeeze a patch of the sheet between her fingers with all her might. She wanted to scream.

Khali gently reached across her torso and took a hold of her tense hand. He massaged it under his own until Gabriana released the threads.

She exhaled suppressed air until once again, she felt at ease with the man who was lying there with her.

Gabriana had to stop fighting, at least for the night. She owed that to Khali, and to herself. That was the due justification that she dosed herself with when she decided to relax. With the room calm and quiet, it wasn't too long before Gabriana dozed back off. This time she dreamed nothing.

~ ~ ~

At 2:30am, Scholar's eyes shot open. The room was pitch black all around him, but by the way his heart was racing, he knew what was happening. The streams of blood trickled out of each nostril.

"Man, come on." Scholar's mind started rotating at a rapid speed. He thought that he was talking aloud to himself, but as he turned sideways, he looked right at the jump-off staring at him from his left side. That threw him off. It was Nya.

Her eyes were wide with amazement and confusion. "You're bleed—"

"Aye, you have to go. You have to get out. Get up..."

"What?" She frowned.

"Get up and get out...now!"

Scholar sat up. He took his one fist and shoved his knuckles up into his nostrils as a plug, and with the other hand, he grabbed for Nya's weave.

"Stop! What are you doing?"

"You think I'm playing? Get out!"

Scholar was panicking. No one had ever witnessed his anxiety attacks, so he had to get the broad out the room, quickly.

When it seemed that she wasn't moving fast enough, Scholar began violently shoving her head.

"Stop!" she screamed through raspy vocal chords.

Nya and Scholar both jumped out of the bed.

"What's wrong... what's wrong with you?" She shrieked.

"Get out!"

"Why? Scholar, what's wrong with you?"

Scholar stopped responding as he took off into the bathroom. *Oh, my God!* You stupid or what? What I gotta do, murder you for you to feel me? What did I just say? Leave right now! Grab your trash and bounce!" he hollered through the closed door, referring to the very clothes she had worn to impress him.

Nya was in shock, but she did exactly as she was told. She threw on her clothes and got out of Scholar's room as fast as a human body could maneuver.

When Scholar turned on the bathroom light, the first thing he did was grab a shower towel and wrap it around his waist. He purposely *didn't* look into the mirror that hung over the sink. He just closed his lids down firmly and turned on the faucet. Scholar splashed, flushed and drenched his face with the cold water for several minutes. With his face down in the sink, he finally opened his eyes and witnessed the droplets of blood that were mixing in with the running water. There were speckles of red splattered all along the boarders of the white porcelain, but for the most part, Scholar paid attention to the pink water rinsing down the drain.

80

Scholar grabbed the closest face towel he could reach, dampened it, then placed the wet cloth over his nose. He turned the faucet off, and then took a few more seconds to deliberately breathe in and out until he had calmed down. After another couple of minutes, the bleeding finally stopped.

He huffed as he slung the bloody towel across the bathroom. "Man, why is this happening?"

Scholar returned to the room a bit shaky, but relieved that Nya was gone.

He sat on the edge of the bed, then turned on the lamp next to him. Scholar picked up his cell phone from the nightstand, but didn't dial the number that was in his head right away. He sat there thinking.

Scholar could never tell what brought on the sudden attacks, and he never knew when they would strike—or where. All he knew was that they were occurring more and more frequently. They seemed to be spiraling out of control, right along with the life he was building for himself. He glanced down at the phone in his hand to view his call history. Gabriana hadn't called back. It had been hours since they had last spoken and usually she would have called or text messaged him at some point during the night. But she hadn't. That was strange.

Scholar stood from the bed and poured himself a shot of the Hennessy that was sitting on the nightstand. He was hoping for immediate gratification, but the alcohol was taking too long to affect his blood. So he poured himself another shot and threw that back. Next, he speed-dialed Gabriana's phone.

No answer.

Scholar removed the device from his earlobe and stared at it oddly.

That never happened before. No matter when he called her, she always answered. It had been like that forever in their relationship so Scholar had gotten used to that loyalty. When he called, she always answered, no matter what. Scholar twisted his face and redialed the number.

Still no answer.

He sent her a text saying to call him immediately. After ten minutes, and no response, Scholar called Gabriana twelve more times before packing his bags up. He decided to head to the airport much earlier than he was scheduled for that day. It was Gabriana's birthday, so he was already booked for a morning flight back, but now he wanted to return on a more advanced plane ticket.

Scholar was pissed at Gabriana for not answering his calls. He called his manager to inform him about the change in flights, then called one of his agents to have her rebook his travel arrangements. "It's URGENT!" He exclaimed in her ear. "Make it happen. I'm leaving out as we speak." Before he could tuck his phone away, Scholar flew out of the hotel room like Batman.

It had been over two *long* months, and suddenly, he desperately wanted to see his girl.

~ ~ ~

"Gabriana, wake up."

Gabriana opened her eyes to the sun-drenched hotel room. Khali stood over the bed, holding her cell phone. "You need to check this because it won't stop buzzing," he said with irritation all over every syllable. Removing the phone from his hand, she reviewed her seventeen missed calls. *Scholar.*

Gabriana returned his call immediately.

"Man, where you at?" he asked loudly. Khali could hear him clearly through the receiver.

"Huh?" Was all Gabriana could say.

"I'm in town and I'm at your..." Scholar's breath delayed a moment before resuming in a vicious grit. "...mother's house." He was seething. Gabriana wasn't sure what had him sounding upset. Was there some kind of serious altercation between himself and Jannette, or did Scholar know something? Gabriana wasn't certain, but she could smell the smoke from his ears through their wireless connection. The sirens in her gut were definitely ringing the alarm. "She said you haven't been here." His baritone rose again. "Where are you?"

Gabriana sat up and cleared her throat. "I'm over at Ciona's house," she lied. "I'll meet you at your house in thirty minutes. Scholar, when—"

Scholar hung up before Gabriana could say another word.

Removing herself quickly from the bed, she caught eye contact with Khali. He was gathering his stuff and preparing to leave. Gabriana wrapped the sheet securely around her body, grabbed her pants off the floor, and walked toward Khali. But he turned away from her and walked out of the hotel room. Gabriana's mouth hung open for a second or two, but she regained her composure. "Whatever, you better get over it," she mumbled.

It was back to business.

At 11:40pm, Gabriana and Scholar pulled up to the private club. It had been advertised all day via radio that the spot would be open to the public. This was per Scholar's request and the place was packed. Everyone in the city knew that this was a Scholar event and they were all on the bandwagon. The club's management took full advantage of the opportunity by charging outrageous door fees. But no one seemed to care. They wanted to see Scholar, and even his girlfriend, in person.

Scholar and Gabriana pulled up to Club Renaissance in her brand new BMW. It was a sparkling royal blue color with a convertible top. Scholar had presented her with the surprise the moment she met him back at his house earlier that day. It was her birthday gift from him. One thing about Scholar was he never forgot his girl's birthday, nor anything material she'd ever expressed interest in. Gabriana wore a dark-blue bubble dress, designed by Rachel Roy. Her gladiator heels were black leather with metallic rocker studs. The clutch purse she carried matched perfectly. She was feeling good and looking her best. She had chosen the outfit carefully. She wanted to complement her new ride, as well as camouflage what little weight she had picked up since she had last seen Scholar. After handing the keys to the valet attendant, a smiling Gabriana was up on her man so tough he could barely walk.

Scholar had reserved the biggest VIP section in the club. Everyone from their crew that could fit was squeezed up in that section. They were all having a ball. Scholar bought out the upstairs bar and ordered one bottle of what seemed like everything for their table. He popped expensive champagne all night in honor of Gabriana. The groupies flooded everywhere. They were wall-to-wall trying to get a glimpse of Scholar. A drunk Gabriana sat on his lap with her arms wrapped securely around his neck as he and his friends made a lot of noise. They were drawing a lot of attention. The music was blazing. Through the thick smoke and the sea of party-goers, Gabriana somehow looked up and caught eye contact with a man standing far, near the back stairway in front of the emergency exit door. He looked very young, but with mature features. Unable to initially break the eye contact, Gabriana blinked her eyes until she was able to turn her head. He made her feel weird. She looked up at Toree who was now standing over her and Scholar.

"Girl, come with me to the bathroom," Scholar's sister insisted. Gabriana poked out her bottom lip and leaned her head down into Scholar's neck. Inhaling his scent, she did not want to leave his side for a second.

"Girl, get up! I want you to get out of this section for at least a minute, you look clingy," Toree yelled through the loud music. She was now getting an attitude.

"Go 'head, Gabri, it's cool," Scholar told her. She kissed his lips and then reluctantly followed Toree.

On the way to the restroom, the groupies seemed to be watching her. Some of them chickens even had the audacity to bump into her as she and Toree squeezed their way through the crowd.

"Aye, these chicks can get it if they really want it. Do I need to swing a bottle or something?" Gabriana said loudly to Toree. She was getting beyond agitated with the hate.

"You know what? You are absolutely right because the next time gon' be the last time," Toree replied while mean-mugging everything moving. The ladies were exhausted from just making it to the restroom, and now they were forced to endure the never-ending line.

Almost twenty minutes later, Gabriana and Torree emerged from the bathroom. A little frustrated but renewed, they made their way back toward the VIP section. As they squeezed through the crowd, Gabriana's heart began to race out of the blue. Taking in a deep breath in the process of pushing her way on, Gabriana felt someone tightly grab a hold of her right arm. It was as if the loud music and the noise of the crowd faded into the background as she looked up at the *man*. His hand squeezed the bare flesh of her arm and she could feel every detail. She felt all the dents, the lines, the flesh, the temperature, every vein and the liquid flowing within his hand. Gabriana felt for only a second that nothing else mattered as she watched the man's mouth when he spoke, "Fear not," before opening his hand and releasing her.

Frightened and confused, she pushed Toree forward, knocking her into a group stuck in the crowd before them. A few people stumbled and some wildly began pushing back. Gabriana blanked out and pushed Toree again, this time even harder. She heard Toree cursing and she heard some people yelling, but her ears felt clogged. She felt the shoves and she felt herself shoving, but ultimately she was detached. The feeling she was experiencing was surreal and indescribable. Suddenly, through the chaos, Gabriana felt Brick grab her around her waist. She felt his hand on her backside, feeling around inappropriately, but she did nothing. Then she saw the bouncers with the flashlights, clearing her way as both Brick and Toree brought her through. Back to the crowded, but more reserved comfort of her VIP area, Gabriana sat down as her vision began to clear. The reality of the sounds around her started to return and the pace of her beating heart began to slowly return to normal. Toree handed her a bottle of water.

"Are you okay?" she asked her, looking concerned.

"What in the world just happened?" Gabriana inquired, shaking her head side to side.

Toree started screaming about the crowd that had pushed them around. Halfway listening to the explanation, the reality of sound began to fail Gabriana again as she glanced around the area. "Where is Scholar?" she asked Toree. She didn't care about what Toree was saying or the fact that she had just interrupted her. Not even waiting for Toree's answer, Gabriana stood and glanced around. There were so many people. No Scholar. Frantically, she left her section and headed out into the crowd again. *Where is he?* She was staring into all kinds of faces, except the right one. Finally spotting one of his bodyguards, Gabriana asked him where was Scholar. The bouncer hesitated before telling her that Scholar and a few members from their entourage had headed downstairs to the lower level of the club.

Finally making her way down to the dim exclusive lower level, Gabriana walked right past the security guards posted near the rope that secured the entrance. They didn't even trip. As she turned the curved trail, and headed toward the group of people in the smoky room ahead, she saw her man. The lights were red, and so was the suede couch that he was perched on.

Scholar had two women slithered all over him. Gabriana watched in disbelief as the bright-skinned, blonde woman slid a hand into Scholar's unbuckled pants. He tilted his head back and closed his eyes. Gabriana's eyes began to sting as she watched on. The second redbone with the boyish haircut also straddled Scholar, sitting closely behind the first whore. She removed Blondie's hand, and then placed her own sticky fingers into the opening of his jeans. She was very tactful with her pleasing him and Scholar lost it. The expression on his face proved that he loved every minute of it. As he rested there on his elbows, moaning, his friends were smiling and cheering the other strippers on. Thick marijuana smoke and naked women were everywhere. At that dark moment, Gabriana saw painfully clear how sick her boyfriend could be. All she could do was stand there like Michael Myers from the horror movie, *Halloween.*

Oh, so this nigga wanna be slick? I should stab everybody down here.

Gabriana remained in place until suddenly, Scholar roamed his lazy sight and caught view of her.

Busted!

Chapter 10

Fuming wasn't even the word. Gabriana didn't know how she squeezed through the crowd so quickly. Arriving back at the table to retrieve her items, she felt the tears burning her eyes. "Enough," she said aloud. Toree wasn't in sight, so Gabriana made her way toward the exit. Briefly looking around, for some strange reason, she found herself looking for that strange *man*. *Ughh.*

Gabriana snatched her keys from the valet attendant. The young white man just shook it off and told her to have a good night. Gabriana flipped him off and hopped in her ride. Feeling lightheaded, her vision blurred. Not even caring, she lowered the top on the BMW and swerved off. After flying through the first two stoplights, Gabriana decided to stop at the third. She reached over to grab her Nas CD from the passenger seat then looked up. She squinted her eyes in disbelief. "Man, what the…?"

The street was oddly empty. The *man* crossed the street and walked in the direction of the BMW. Gabriana was frozen. He seemed to be moving very quickly toward her. Once the *man* got within a foot of the car, Gabriana put the pedal to the floor.

"Gabriana." She heard him shout her name, but strangely his voice was not loud.

Why was this man stalking her? Gabriana played the rerun in her head as she drove forward. He was a very handsome man, but again, she could not tell his age. The more she thought about it, she couldn't even describe his race. "Who is that, and how in the world did he know my name?" she asked aloud. Gabriana bust a U-turn and returned down the same desolate street. She was headed back toward the *man*. This time there were a few cars around as she slowly crept down the street. Looking left and right, Gabriana could not find *him*. After turning down a few more streets with no sight of him, Gabriana gave up and headed back toward Scholar's house.

How did he get away so fast? That is so weird.

Back at the house, Gabriana laid down in the empty bedroom. The house was completely quiet. It was going on 4:00am and Scholar hadn't returned. She had been back at his house for over an hour, and he still hadn't called. Scholar hadn't even sent a text message. Gabriana's burnt eyes swirled around the large bedroom. She took in all the candles that laced every piece of furniture that could hold them. Scholar had placed them there. He told Gabriana that they were for her. He said that they were symbolic of how much he thought about her while they were apart. *Game*! Gabriana knew that, but the thought was still sweet.

In addition to all of the gifts that afternoon, Scholar had completely cleared out his house. There was to be no one there, but him and her. But alone with him, Gabriana was a nervous wreck. There was so much on her mind that she wondered if her smile was giving off the illusion of being forced. She didn't want Scholar to trip, so she moved feverishly around the house, just making up things to do. That helped out for a little while, but it didn't continue on for much longer. Scholar had gotten out of the shower and called for her to come into his bedroom. Gabriana knew what was next, and there was no escaping it.

Usually, Gabriana was more anxious for her dude, but at that time she was worried sick. She was afraid that he would *know*. Before she met up with Scholar, Gabriana had gone back to her mother's house to soak and scrub any and all evidence of Khali off of her body. But she couldn't rinse him out of her soul that easily. It hadn't been a full twenty-four hours since she had been with another man, and that just felt wrong. Gabriana's heart went down into her stomach. Or her stomach went up into her heart. Whichever it was, it made her feel nauseated. She didn't know what to expect, so she was flipping inside, but Scholar had a surprise for her.

Scholar didn't light one candle in that room. He told Gabriana that they were for later that night. She asked him if he wanted her to go change into the new lingerie he had purchased for her, but Scholar just laughed. "Nah, save all that for after we hit the club up tonight. The only thing I want on you is me." He then took her into his arms.

It was apparent on Scholar's face. He only wanted her—his Gabri— and nothing else at the moment. So she gave herself up.

Every apprehension and doubt that Gabriana walked in that room with hit the wind. Everything dissipated within her soul. Scholar was so into her that it scared her. She never questioned his desire for her, but something extra was on display during their moment. Not only did he tell her back to back to back that he loved her, but judging by the way he handled Gabriana, he really missed her as well. Once he finally allowed her the freedom to crawl out of his bed, Gabriana had collapsed onto the floor the second she tried to stand. She was being silly, but in actuality, Scholar had successfully made an extreme point of whatever validity he felt he had to demonstrate. They both found that hilarious. After she finally got it together, Gabriana was floating. Scholar had re-broken her all the way down in the few hours since he had returned. He made sure his placement was solidified, and she was completely re-convinced that this was the man for her. Forget Khali, and any other guy, or person for that matter. Her man was back. When they'd left for Gabriana's party, she was so excited, and anticipating the long hours ahead with her favorite dude in the world, but now, she had returned—all alone.

In need of some attention, Gabriana dialed Khali's number. She knew it was late, but it was the weekend, and she really wanted to talk to him right then. The voicemail picked up after the fourth ring. She wanted to leave a message, but instead, she pressed *End*. Gabriana decided to send a text to Khali. She wrote:

~ *Baby, pls give me a call. I need 2 talk to u asap! If you can, pls, I want to come over…wherever you are, I want to come.* ~

Thirty minutes later, there was still no reply from Khali. "Maybe he's sleep," she said in between sobs. Gabriana rarely cried, but it seemed that Scholar had really been pulling it out of her lately. "Scholar, why dude? What is going on? Tell me what I am doing wrong," she cried out before falling off into a deep sleep.

~~~

Once Renaissance let out, Scholar had to catch a ride home with his bodyguards, Jason and Bear. There were so many females trying to leave with him that his entourage made riot-like noises, saluting him outside the club. Still, Scholar wasn't that crazy. He knew he had to get home; He was in enough trouble. Scholar didn't like the fact that Gabriana had to see what she saw, but it was what it was. There wasn't any sense in running out behind her because there was nothing that he would have been able to say. He was caught with his hand in the cookie jar, doing the things that he had been doing on a regular basis when she wasn't around. Running behind his chick, trying to explain something he couldn't would have only caused an unwanted scene. "She shouldn't have followed me, she asked to see that." He tried to justify his actions to his conscious by reversing the fault. "She'll get over it. I'll make sure she do. I'll make it up to her."

Midway through the ride, Scholar was twisted, but not enough to drown out the sounds that came flooding throughout the Maserati SUV. This was his own transportation, which he was courteous enough to let niggas pull out for stunting, but yet, he couldn't control the music. Bear was the self-proclaimed deejay and he wasn't in the "mood" for any more rap music. He needed to mellow down.

Scholar had no problem with the R&B singer, Usher, but his CD, *Confessions,* was not the exact kind of lyrics he was trying to hear while heading home. Especially the song, "Simple Things." Those lyrics had him subconsciously frowned up, and thinking. The singer brought reality to his distorted mind.

Nigga, what's wrong with you? You've been trippin'.

It wasn't just the guilt of the night, but the guilt of staying away so long, and the guilt of pacifying his woman with material things. He knew Gabriana wanted more of his time, but that didn't justify why she had lied to him earlier. In all honesty, deep within, that was the true reason why he had played her at her own party. He really couldn't get over the insecure feeling that she had caused him by uncharacteristically not answering his calls, then lying about her whereabouts. He wasn't naïve like her. Scholar knew absolutely well that Gabriana wasn't at Ciona's crib overnight. Those chicks didn't even talk anymore.

That afternoon, Scholar waited impatiently for Gabriana's arrival. An additional two hours had passed from the thirty minutes she'd said it would take her to reach his home. Scholar called her repeatedly, but she had stopped answering her phone again. She would only text him sporadically, saying she was on her way. Eventually, she had made it to him, but to his surprise, Gabriana didn't come into the house. She called him from the front yard where she stood awaiting him.

When he went out to meet her, Scholar was expecting to see this dolled-up version of his girl, but instead, Gabriana was all natural and baby fresh. She seemed cleansed. She wore only a white sequined tee under a thin pink hoodie, which she covered with a soft blackberry leather jacket. Washed-over J-Brand jeans rode her hips low, but only a pair of simple short folk boots graced her feet. There were no accessories adorning her, and absolutely no makeup on Gabriana's face. Not even lip gloss. Her lips were naturally smoothed with Chap Stick as she looked upon him through black wide-rimmed glasses. Her hair was not straightened how he usually preferred it, but pulled into a curly bushy ponytail. Scholar studied her before fully making an approach.

The first thing he had done was put his hands to her hair, and removed the band. He wanted to see her hair down. The curls and wavy strands felt damp as they poured down over her shoulders and his hands. He pulled her into his embrace and sniffed atop her crown. In combination with Pomegranate-Berry body wash, the strong scent of shampoo overwhelmed Scholar's senses. It was as if this girl had soaked in soapy bathe water for an hour. Her simplicity was infant-like, and with the pink hooded jacket, and prescription glasses, which she rarely wore, she appeared more youthful, and more innocent than ever. Scholar's heart had skipped a beat when he removed the glasses from Gabriana's face. He wanted to see her eyes clearly, and what he saw was a film of clear liquid. Gabriana broke their stare first by looking down, then placing her face into Scholar's chest. He felt the vibrations of her shoulders as she silently sobbed. "Dude, I missed you so much. I missed you so much." she gently cried to him.

Scholar had no response. He held her close for a minute, then pulled her slightly back to kiss her forehead, then her lips. Gabriana tried to wipe her tears away with the back of her hand, but Scholar removed it. He placed his own hand on her cool cheek and felt the warm tears for himself. Feeling at fault, he pecked both of her cheeks several times then pulled Gabriana into a cuddle.

"Don't cry, Gabri. Listen to me, I'm sorry I left you. I won't do that again. I promise. I'm going to take care of you, that's my word. Everything's gonna be all right. Everything's gonna be straight. I promise."

Scholar felt guilty for leaving her alone for months. It was easy for him to cut her tears short over the phone, but in person, this was his baby. His heart fell weak the second he'd looked at Gabriana, and he wanted to make it all right again. That was possible. With all the money he had spent for this day, Scholar knew inside that it would only be a few more minutes before her smile would return. But he still had questions, and a feeling that needed to be addressed.

Scholar took Gabriana into the house. Just as he knew she would be, Gabriana was astonished to see the large Caribbean lunch that he had catered and setup for her delight. There was a load of food spread about on beautiful pearl and wood dishes. Gabriana eyed everything in awe. There was Jerk chicken, brown rice, cabbage, plantains and oxtail soup. All of it looked wonderful, but the center piece of all the grandiosity displayed, was the elaborate papaya birthday cake, frosted with European Wray and Nephew Rum icing, otherwise known as the most expensive rum in the world.

In addition, surrounding the dessert sat twelve coconut-laced flutes of Mimosa. Gabriana was momentarily speechless. Once her tongue came back to life, all she could say was, "All of this is for us?"

Scholar replied, "Nah, all of this is for *you*. And still, it's not enough." He knew she probably charged his statement to game, but he actually meant every word. Aside from what was bothering him, he did want to see her enjoy her birthday exclusively at his expense. He felt he owed her that much.

Scholar had fed Gabriana samples of every dish in sight before personally preparing plates for their dining. After getting full on food, the two of them talked awhile, but Scholar was antsy. "Follow me, Gabriana. I have a gift for you."

A few minutes later, Scholar had walked Gabriana around the back to the large garage, then handed over the keys to the BMW M3 Drop-Top. She screamed like an opera singer and hugged him around his neck. That was on point, because while she was within eardrum reach, Scholar took the opportunity to ask her softly, "Why did you lie to me?"

Then everything switched at the speed of light.

"Huh?"

Scholar hadn't repeated a word. Instead, he had released himself from the embrace, and looked Gabriana directly in the eyes. His expression was supreme and stern. His eyes were like laser beams.

"Keon, what are you talking about?" Gabriana's voice had shook with seriousness. On top of that, she'd called him by his government name. She only did that when the pressure was on. Scholar knew what time it was. He knew he had her.

"You lied to me about where you were. Where were you at, Gabriana? Don't—"

"I told—"

"Don't lie to me." Scholar's voice rose so he caught himself, and lowered it. This caused his next words to come out as a determined grit. "I know you, I know you're lying to me."

Gabriana had tilted her head slightly over and frowned up the sides of her lips with disgust. "You have got to be kidding me." She pointed a stiff index finger at his nose. "If I told you that I was with Ciona, then *THAT'S* where I was. Don't come at me like that, Scholar. If you hadn't been gone for *TWO* whole months then you would have known that we'd been in touch. You would have—"

"You would have mentioned that! You act like we didn't talk at all, Gabriana. I know you would have mentioned that this longtime missing "homegirl" of yours was back in the picture. I don't believ—"

"What are you saying? Are you saying that you don't trust me?" Gabriana had asked him through her teeth. "Because if you are, then you might as well spit up the name of the female that *you* were with last night. Because you're guilty of something."

At that point, Scholar was ready to drop it. She looked and acted serious enough. Maybe he was tripping. Plus, he wasn't trying to get into any discussions about his own actions. All Scholar could do was take her word for it. Besides, he didn't want to ruin all the surprises he had in store for her.

As the truck breezed through the night, the cool air that blew in through the cracked windows sobered Scholar. Usher continued to sing more question marks into his head while all the ways which he had been mistreating and neglecting his lady, were playing visuals. Scholar knew the conclusion. He had to make things right, and he was well-prepared to do so. He just had to get himself mentally prepped.

~ ~ ~

"Happy birthday, Gabriana," each person would say as they walked by her on the street. Gabriana never replied, she just continued to walk. The sky was darkened with an overcast of clouds, but there was no wind. She approached the gray-colored brick monastery. Gabriana walked right past the wide-stoned steps and continued on until she reached the side of the building. She glanced up at a large window. The man stood next to her. She knew who he was, but she never looked over at him. She just continued to stare up at the window. Gabriana could see his form in her peripheral view. He spoke to her softly saying, "Fear not, Gabriana."

Gabriana never opened her mouth. She replied with her mind. "I'm afraid, I don't want to be alone."

The man was silent. Gabriana spoke again in her mind. "Speak to me, stranger. Who are you and what do you want with me? I need to see in that window up there." The stranger said to her, "I will not tell you my name, it is not important, but I do have a message to give you. Do you want to hear?"

Gabriana didn't answer right away. She slowly looked over her shoulder, but never at the stranger. "Yes," she finally replied in her mind. The stranger said, "Many will come and many will go. Do not be afraid... there is a plan."

The tears were flowing down Gabriana's cheeks. She asked, "Will Scholar go?"

The stranger replied gently. "Yes, Gabriana, prepare yourself."

Gabriana didn't remember falling to her knees as she looked up from them. She couldn't speak, she only cried. She didn't see the stranger walk away, but he was gone. In her mind she could hear him say, "Stand." She arose immediately. The next thing Gabriana knew, she was floating high up above the ground. She didn't know how or what was suspending her there. She looked down into the large window of the building. Below, there was a huge empty room. She heard figures moving about in the space, but she saw no one. At the front of the room was a coffin. Gabriana couldn't see the body. She strained her eyes. "Show me," she demanded. The room's view grew larger before her eyes. She stared into the coffin and whispered, "Why?"

The rain was drenching her, as she remained suspended in the air in front of the window. The stranger's voice said, "Fear not, it will be okay."

Suddenly, Gabriana was on her knees again. The rain was pouring so hard that it was blurring her vision. She closed her eyes and thought of the body in the coffin. "Mama, don't leave me please," she screamed.

~ ~ ~

Gabriana opened her eyes. She had a pounding headache. Lifting her phone, she glanced at the pending text. It read:

~ Gabri I'm sorry but I had to catch an early morning flight out to MIA and dnt act like u 4got. U was sleepn so good so I ddnt bother wak'n u. B4 you get 2 trip'n, Im sending 4 u. Book a flight with my agent and get out here as soon as u can baby cuz I want 2 make things rght wit u. Luv u my lady ~ Scholar ~

Chapter 11

Although Jannette practically begged her daughter to stay, Gabriana wasn't thinking straight. She was losing it, and she was losing him, so she boarded that plane anyway.

About twenty minutes into the flight, the lights flickered and her heartbeat began to speed up. "Oh, my God!" Gabriana tried to relax. Five minutes later the plane shook violently with what felt like extreme turbulence. Trying not to panic, Gabriana looked around at the other passengers. Yep, it was time to panic. The passengers began to mumble with fear. The plane shook again, this time it shook harder and longer then before. The flight's staff began frantically moving about the aisles, trying to calm the passengers. Then there was a bump that caused the lights to flicker again. Gabriana closed her eyes. "God, please," she whimpered.

She could hear the fear in the voices around her as the shaking and bumps became persistent. Because her eyes were closed, Gabriana couldn't see the crazy flicker of the lights. The voice of the captain came over the speaker. Gabriana could not understand what he was saying to the passengers because she was speaking to the voice in her head that was whispering, "Fear not."

In her mind, she responded to the voice. "Save me, please."

Gabriana didn't make it into Miami until late the next day. Because of the emergency landing and the reconnecting of flights, she was exhausted. She laid across from Scholar on the bed. As much as she wanted to relax, she couldn't. Scholar was on his cell phone, arguing back and forth with Brick.

"Nothing that you are saying to me matters, so kill it. I'm not hearing you at all, this is my show. What is you talking about, Brick?" *Pause* "Do whatever you feel like you gotta do, I don't care. I don't fear nothing, ever." *Pause* "What you think, I fear you? There ain't no fear in my heart. If that's how you feel, then come see me then. I'm done wit' you 'cuz you petty, nigga!" *Pause* "I been keeping it real since day one, nigga, but you don't understand, so I'm done proving my point and it's whatever. I don't care," Scholar declared in an almost hoarse voice.

Gabriana could hear Brick returning assaults on Scholar through the receiver. She wasn't feeling this. Why were they arguing so much lately? They were supposed to be like brothers. "This is stupid," she said aloud as she lifted herself from the bed and headed for the balcony. Stepping out into the warm air of Miami, she sparked her square. A few minutes later, Scholar joined her.

His light-brown skin was reddish with heat. He lit a cigarette. Gabriana looked over at him, and she could see the tears in the back of his eyes. "Scholar, tell me what's going on? Something is wrong," she gently said to him.

He looked over the balcony, then bit down on his bottom lip. This was his signature trait when in thought. Gabriana expected him to explode, but surprisingly he spoke just as gently as she had. "Everything is wrong," he calmly said.

Surprised by his honesty, she moved closer to him. "Like what? Tell me," she softly urged.

"Baby, niggas is straight hating on me right now and I've been doing everything for everybody." His voice cracked. "Man, that nigga Brick messing up big time. He's a fag fo' real."

102

Gabriana had heard the rumors about Brick and a few other dudes laying their burdens on Scholar. They had been putting pressure on him about everything from writing checks everywhere to laundering all kinds of money and the Feds were on everybody's tongue.

"Yeah, I heard some foul things," she admitted to Scholar.

"Nah, it ain't no secret and that's the problem right there," he said. He flicked his cigarette and looked up at the sky. "I ain't try'na lose everything that I worked for behind these simple-minded niggas. Nah, that can't happen. I'm fed up with this circus and I'm starting to not trust nobody, Gabriana, you hear me?" Scholar said with angry eyes.

Gabriana thought about the night of her birthday at the club when Brick grabbed her from behind. Against her better judgment, she looked at Scholar then confirmed his suspicions. She went ahead and told him what Brick had pulled on her that night.

Big mistake.

Scholar was so mad he kicked the balcony's slide door, shattering it. Glass cubes landed everywhere. Gabriana tried to calm him, but it didn't work. Scholar walked through the room, throwing everything he could get his hands on. He began kicking at the wall and cursing Brick. "He's dead! I swear, I'm going to murder that nigga!" He did not play that game with niggas when it came to his girl and he was enraged to the fullest.

That was Sunday night. By the following Wednesday, Gabriana was just about ready to return home. Scholar's attitude was horrific and he was constantly screaming at her. "I do everything for you," he reminded her. "You are the most ungrateful person I ever met! You need to show more respect! Real talk, I'm not even sure if I can trust *you*."

"Then why are you with me?" She would ask him. Scholar never had an answer for that question. Instead, he would just grab the nearest object he could grab a hold of and throw it. A few times, those objects flew right toward her, forcing her to dodge or duck. Gabriana was full to the rim with Scholar's irate behavior. She wondered what happened to "making things right." The whole reason for coming out to Miami went out the window. Her little confession had backfired entirely.

When Scholar had confronted Brick about the incident with Gabriana, one of the homies came to Brick's defense, telling Scholar that he had witnessed what "really" happened that night. He informed Scholar that Gabriana didn't have a problem with Brick grabbing on her. He told Scholar that she did absolutely nothing in retaliation. To make matters even worse, Toree had confirmed the homie's story. She told her brother, "Yeah, she ain't know that I peeped that, too. If you gone check your boy, you better also check your girl 'cause I know for a fact she isn't innocent."

This planted the seed of distrust within Scholar, so everyday he had been going hard on Gabriana. Daily, he would put her on blast. He meant every letter in the words when he told Gabriana, "I don't want you nowhere near any of my niggas anymore. If I catch you out of line, I'm throwing you out with the garbage, believe that. Straight up, I'm not feeling you right now, so you need to just stay out of my way."

Gabriana just went through the motions everyday during that week. Scholar wouldn't even get in the bed with her until she was already asleep. In the middle of the night, she would wake up and nestle up close to him. This seemed to be the only opportunities available for embracing him. When he would wake, he would remove her limbs from his body then go back to sleep. One of those times, he had actually exited the bed altogether. The tension was becoming too much, so Gabriana packed up her belongings. When Scholar saw this, he unpacked everything and threw her things all around. The site looked like a tornado had blown through it. He told her that she couldn't leave 'til he said so. Gabriana was not allowed to leave the city or the room. Thursday evening, when she left out anyway while he was showering, she returned to an attack that she never saw coming. Now, Scholar had smacked her up before, and he often threatened her, but never had he done the things he did to her that dreadful night.

When she had returned back to the suite, it was only a little after 10:00pm. Gabriana had left to go down to the lobby of the hotel to get a drink. She had simply needed to get out and relieve some stress. She had wanted desperately to talk to Khali or Jannette alone, but as luck would have it, she had left her phone back in the room. After a couple of stiff drinks, Gabriana decided to call it a night. As soon as she stepped foot through the door, Scholar slammed it closed and grabbed her by her throat. He never said a word. He slung her onto the bed and with a closed fist, he hit her. Then he hit her again, and again. It was on.

Gabriana's cry escaped her throat as an animal-like shrill. The tears burst through her sockets as she tried, unsuccessfully, to guard her face.

WHOP...WHOP...WHOP...WHOP...WHOP

The strikes were so forceful that Gabriana's eyesight appeared crooked in her twisted vision. Her view suddenly appeared as if she were seeing things from upside down, and on top of that, every colorful thing around looked like smeared paint. Scholar picked up speed as he began to use both fists to repeatedly bang on her. He pounded the sides of Gabriana's head, ears, and face like a maniac. Her bones crackled under each strike. The more she tried to cover up, the harder Scholar swung. She tried to turn away, but that move only resulted in him viciously attacking her forehead. When Gabriana pushed her arms up to block that area, that's when she felt the stinging blow to her nose. Then everything turned from runny colors to black and white.

The blood leaked onto the bed and then onto the carpet as she rolled down to the floor. Gabriana was facedown and choking. The pain was unbearable. Scholar hit her again in the back of her head. The blow was so hard that her face crashed down into the plush carpet. Gabriana couldn't think, and she couldn't hear. Her ears began to ring. When she turned onto her side to grab a hold of her ears, Scholar grabbed her long hair and violently snatched her onto her back. He then began banging her head on the carpeted floor while screaming something down on her. The floor no longer felt like carpet, it felt like steal. Every time her head knocked the floor, Gabriana's brain shifted, and her nose exploded. The blood gushed from each nostril. With all her strength, she tried to sit up, but Scholar pushed his hand and forearm down harshly on her face. The watch on his wrist carved down into her cheek, splitting the skin.

He's trying to kill me... I'm going to die... I'm going to die...

Gabriana's head and body were vibrating from the inside out. "Sch... Scholar. Please, no more, please...please," she begged uselessly. She didn't even realize that she was babbling the words because she was so dazed.

"No...No...let my shirt go, Gabriana! Let me go...you wanna lie to me..."

WHOP...WHOP!

Gabriana didn't realize that she had grabbed the collar of Scholar's T-shirt and was stretching it. It was an obsolete defense, but it was the most she could do. Once the licks ceased, she released his shirt. Her eyes were barely opened when she peeped out her skull and saw the barrel of the gun pointing directly in her face. Then for a split second she could hear again.

"I should *kill* you. I should blow out your brains right here."

Gabriana wanted to protest, but she couldn't. She knew it was all over for her. All she could do was hold her breath. With the contributing help of Scholar's free hand pressing and squeezing severely down on her neck, Gabriana's constricted windpipes finally faulted, and she blacked out. The brutality finally ended.

After cleansing the blood off of himself, Scholar left the hotel room and rushed down the hall toward the elevators. He pounded his index finger into the control button endlessly until the doors slid open. The inside was empty and he couldn't have been more appreciative. As the elevator descended downward, Scholar held his head up and away from the surrounding mirrors. It seemed as if time was standing still and suddenly he felt trapped inside the elevator. For only a brief moment, he looked ahead into one of the mirrors.

Scholar searched his face for some form of sanity. The familiar features that he was used to admiring in the mirror were missing. The reflection that looked back through the glass before him was not Keon, but his father. Scholar gasped then squinted his eyes at the mirror. Before the frightful sight could torture him any farther, he doubled over with pain as the cramps ripped through his stomach and abdominal area. His body felt like hundreds of small bombs were exploding within him. Everything inside of him was erupting and he needed to find someone, but who? Scholar tried to look anywhere but into one of those mirrors again. There was nowhere else to look and no one to turn to. As a means of distraction, he hastily pulled out one of his cell phones to look at the screen.

Twenty-one missed calls from Brick.

"Back up, nigga! *Back up*! I don't trust you. I don't trust nobody,"

Scholar yelled out. "God...God please..." he frantically tried to plead.

The stomach pains stabbed at him again. This time, the intensity of the cramps caused him to yelp out instead of completing his pending prayer. Not wanting to fall out, he leaned his weight back against the glass wall behind him. He closed his eyes to find *somebody* to pray to, but the bell dinged and the doors of the cage opened.

Scholar rushed off the elevator and walked briskly into the lobby of the hotel. There were a few people hanging around and they surely took notice of the distraught-looking young star. Just as Scholar was about to step into the revolving doors that led to outside, he froze up, and could not move. He stood there with his hands on top of his head. His palms brushed harshly forward and backward over the low waves of his hair.

Go back upstairs.

"No, NEVER!" he exclaimed to the voice in his head.

More people stopped to look. "Sir, are you okay?"

"Excuse me?"

"You're not looking well. Do you need some help?" someone else asked.

The voices were popping up all around. Then, when the man with the dreadlocks lifted a Smartphone up to sneak a snapshot, that was Scholar's cue to get out of there. His eyes felt like there was acid in them, and he knew that he probably looked alarmingly upset, but there was nothing he could do about it. He could not hide his feelings this time. They were hurting him too badly. Without responding to any of the random voices speaking to him, Scholar hit the doors.

Once he made his way through the exit, and was safely outside,

Scholar tried to gather himself. That's when an old bag lady spoke to him from behind. "Sir, do you have any spare change?"

"What?" Scholar turned around and looked the woman up and down. "What?" He repeated.

The old woman smiled with her eyes and stuck out her hands. They cupped together as if someone was going to pour water into them. Scholar couldn't believe the way everything was spinning. He shut his eyes for a moment. It all seemed surreal, and for the first time in a very long time, he felt absolutely confused and alone. He needed to get to his car. Just as Scholar was about to walk away, the old woman said, "Go make it right, baby. It's okay; just go make it right."

Scholar flipped. He spun around in the direction of the bum and screamed at her, "What?! What do you need, money?!" He snatched a stack of twenties and fifties out his pocket. "Here, take this twenty and get away from me, a'ight? Just mind your business and don't say nothing else to me."

The woman took the bill and noticed that it was not a twenty at all, but a fifty. When Scholar tried to walk away again, she grabbed the back of his shirt, causing him to instinctively snatch roughly away. "Don't touch me...don't ever touch me!"

"But you gave me a fifty by mistake. Here take this back," she tried to tell him, but he started walking off in the opposite direction again. That's when she shouted out, "You need to stop and focus."

Scholar stopped in the middle of his steps and turned around again to face the lady. "Wha...? What did you say to me?"

"Nothing," the woman murmured.

"Nah, yes you did. Repeat it for me," Scholar said as he walked up on her. The disbelieving and sinister look on his face caused the woman to slightly back up.

"I said...I said focus," she suddenly repeated. That old woman didn't know why she was saying what she was saying. The words were just forming on her tongue by default.

That next thing that everyone watching saw was Scholar smack the bag lady in the face with all the bills in his hand. The money made a swoop and flap sound as the bills hit her face and then floated all around. Her eyes were huge as full moons, and she wanted to react, but there was nothing else for her to say.

Scholar's eyes watched the lady with intense anger, then he tried to shake it off. He didn't mean to do her like that, but his being couldn't respond any other way. In actuality, he didn't mean to do his girlfriend how he had just done her either. Back in that room, he had completely spazzed out on Gabriana and the damage was done. He didn't know how to react to everything he was feeling, or anything that was going on. He didn't understand any part of anything anymore. He never did, really. There was a wave of chaos and voices were going crazy inside of his spirit. Something was going on that he couldn't handle alone, but since he felt betrayed by everyone, he was going to have to deal with it solo. Scholar was feeling stripped of all control. So everything about him started to shut down all things, including his focus. His eyes became dim, and his sight became blurry.

Scholar headed toward the garage to pull out his car. As he carelessly crossed into the street he heard someone in his head speak again.

Go back inside.

"Nah, I can't," he replied out loud. Scholar's voice was becoming hoarse with each word. The emotion he was feeling regarding his girl-friend was like a rising volcano lava.

"I can't do that. I'm gone... it's over. She don't love me. She don't love me at all." Scholar didn't realize that he was wiping away tears with the bottom of his palm as he talked to himself, or whoever it was that was speaking to him in his spirit. He was spaced out and assumed the wetness was sweat.

In that next moment, Scholar's cell phone rang. He removed it from his pocket and looked down at the caller ID.

It was Brick again. Scholar didn't hesitate to hit *Ignore* for the ump-teenth time on that nigga. Once that call was sent to voicemail, he dialed his bodyguard Jason's number.

"I'm on my way over there," he told Jason as he headed inside and down the lower level of the parking garage.

"A'ight. You sounding all urgent, though. Where's Bear? You by your-self? What's up? Are you good?"

"Nah, I'm not. I just beat..." Scholar paused before continuing. He needed to catch his breath. "Almost murdered... Everything is... I'm los-ing my mind right now, dawg."

"Scholar, what are trying to say? What happened?" Jason flooded the questions out.

"I just told you. I'm losing my mind right now. She's gonna call the police, I know it. I'm going to jail, dawg."

"What the—?"

111

"Look, just be looking out. I'm on my way. I'm heading to my car right now. Be looking out."

"A'ight...a'ight. Come on through, bruh. Calm down, I got you. I'm right here," the husky baritone on the other end assured. Scholar didn't say anything else; he just disconnected the call.

~ ~ ~

All day Friday, Gabriana stayed locked up in the room, crying and throwing up, until she could not anymore. Her stomach muscles produced convulsions throughout her entire body. The extreme lightheaded-effect was equivalent to the spells one experiences after popping multiple Percocet pills. The dizziness would not subside. She felt so sick. Uncontrollably, she shivered and dry-heaved. Over and over she would go to the mirror and examine the multiple dark bruises and lumps about her head and face. It took hours for Gabriana's hearing to return to her right ear. That same side of her face was so swollen that she could only slightly open her mouth. It had taken her a full thirty minutes just to brush her teeth that morning. Gabriana was devastated. "It hurts. It hurts so bad. Why would he do this?" she cried out to her reflection.

Her spirit ached worse than her body. The physical damage done was nowhere in comparison to the inner damage which Scholar had marked her with. She felt much worse then she looked. With trembling hands, Gabriana looked all around the room for her phone, but the search was in vain. While she laid unconscious, and abandoned, on the floor the night before, Scholar had taken her phone before he left. He had not returned or made any attempts to check on her since. Alone in the room, Gabriana stood over the bloodstain on the carpet. Her intent was to begin cleaning up the mess. Instead, she broke out into a frenzy. Her soul was heavy and her head was blazing. She didn't know if her brain was hemorrhaging because the headache was so atrocious. When Gabriana couldn't cry any more vigorously, she got on her knees and prayed. She prayed harder than she ever had in her life. Out of every tear she shed in that prayer, and out of every word she uttered, not one of those words were on her behalf. They were all for Scholar.

Gabriana prayed that God would forgive him.

Chapter 12

Saturday morning, Gabriana arose early. She actually felt better after that prayer. After a long shower, she wrapped the thick towel around her and walked across the room to turn on the radio. Everything in the room seemed brighter that day. The last week had been hell for her, but for some reason, today seemed like a new day.

Gabriana was fully dressed and sitting on the bed in deep thought when Scholar walked in. She looked up at him and immediately became stiff with thick emotion.

"Where are you going, Gabriana?" he asked her in a low voice. He kept his head lowered to the floor as if he was afraid to face her.

"Look at me, Scholar," she calmly said to him. Scholar didn't reply. He walked over to the bed and sat down next to her, but he didn't say anything, and never looked at her.

"Who are you?" she asked him. "Do you even know who I am?"

Silence

Gabriana reached over to grab his face, but he knocked her hands from him and turned away.

"Scholar," she said with a trembling voice.

No answer.

"Scholar, look at me." Still there was no answer. She wanted him to view the bruises and the full aftermath of his violent assault. She sat on his left, but he kept his head turned to the right.

Before she could stop what overcame her, Gabriana stood and punched Scholar in the side of his face as hard as she could. "You are a punk, nigga. I *HATE* you," she shrieked with intensity so raw that it burned her throat. She then swung on him again.

Scholar quickly stood and grabbed her arms, so she began kicking him. "You want to know where I'm going, you FAG? I'm going home and I never want to see you again," she screamed, trying to escape his hold. Scholar spun her around and pushed her down on the bed. He then forced her backward and laid his weight on top of her. Gabriana was pushing, kicking and screaming. When she tried to claw his face, he then pinned her arms above her head. She struggled for her freedom. "Let me go, punk! You don't trust me. You don't love me. I hate you. *I HATE YOUR GUTS!*"

Scholar never replied. He just rolled off of her and tried to speak, but began choking. Gabriana froze instantly. Scholar continued to try to speak, but the tears wouldn't allow him to breathe. The only words that she could make out were, "You said…"

Gabriana was totally in shock at that point because never, ever had she seen him cry like that. Matter of fact, she had never seen him cry, period. Scholar sat up on the bed and slid forward to the edge. He continued to cry like a baby. Gabriana was silent. After a full two minutes of watching Scholar's breakdown, she stood and backed away from the bed.

"Look at me, Scholar." Fresh tears were now falling from her eyes, but she didn't realize it. When Scholar finally looked into her face, he quickly turned away. In that instant, Gabriana was able to catch a glimpse of the guilt his eyes held before he could quickly divert them back to the wall. He pulled the bottom of his T-shirt up over his face and started crying again. The thin fabric he held up failed to muffle the distressed sobs. With his free hand, Scholar grabbed his stomach as if he was in excruciating pain. His entire body was twisted and rocked - rocked and twisted.

"Look at me, Keon," Gabriana said so low that she didn't think he heard her, but he had. Removing the shirt from his red face, he looked up at her again. Both Gabriana and Scholar stared at each other. Although his chest heaved desperately for air, the emotion halted as they stared on. That was the moment when Gabriana saw something that sent chills through her very core. She saw much more than guilt this time. It was like she was looking at a child. She couldn't describe the look on Scholar's face, even if someone had offered to pay her a million dollars for the description. *Something was deeply wrong here.*

The room was silent. Scholar stood. With his breathing slightly calmer, he wiped his face with the bottom of his shirt and then headed for the door. As he passed Gabriana, he paused at her right side and bore his eyes into the side of her face. Gabriana never turned her head to face him directly as he stood there. He was so close, and she wanted desperately to touch him, but her entire body was suspended. Her mind and heart reached for him, but physically she did not budge. Scholar opened his mouth to speak, but the only sound that came out was a whimper. Huffed. Tears began to stream down again. They dripped freely off the bottom of his jaws. With his right hand, he wiped the moisture off his face, then placed it into his right pants pocket, and removed a closed fist. He then opened his fist and released the ring, it fell to the floor. It landed near Gabriana's foot. Neither of them looked down at it. Scholar moved toward the door again. Before reaching for the knob, he roared, "*GABRI!*" That was the only sound heard. The incomplete word thundered out and gave effect to his true feeling. Although he could not complete her entire name, his displeasure was well felt. And dramatically expressed. Scholar banged the bottom of his fist on the door.

Gabriana jumped from the sudden noise, but could not bring herself to move from her stance. She stood still with her back to him. When she heard the door open, Gabriana forced the words, "Scholar, stop," out of her throat. But he didn't. Maybe her response was too dry for his theatrics. The only response she received in return, was the click of the door closing. There was no loud slam. It just gently shut. Ending...something. Still standing frozen, Gabriana whispered out into the emptiness. This time the words floated from her insides without stinging. "I don't hate you. I love you." Suddenly her already hot blood felt feverish and something literally spoke within her.

Go after him and tell him you love him.

But she didn't. Anger and pride held her captive.

~ ~ ~

Gabriana paid the taxi driver the fee, plus a tip. Moving slowly, she wheeled her luggage forward. The time was 7:01pm. Her flight wasn't due to leave until 9:15pm. She was extremely early, but because Scholar never returned to the suite, Gabriana left. She sat there for hours, thinking about him after he left out of the door. The most beautiful custom-made engagement ring she had ever seen twirled between her fingertips the entire time as she sat and waited. She wanted to call him, but he never gave her phone back. Gabriana could have used the room's landline phone, but she just didn't. She simply let it go. She was too confused.

Gabriana entered one of the airport lobby's Bar and Grill restaurants. She hadn't eaten a thing for almost two days and she still had no appetite. Feeling lightheaded, she decided on some chips and salsa.

Thirty minutes later, she was still nibbling on that same appetizer. The Italian bartender asked Gabriana if she wanted a drink. Removing her sunglasses, she answered, "Actually, yes. I will take a Remy Martin straight-up."

The bartender stared at Gabriana's bruises a little too long for her liking. "Are you going to judge me, or go fix my drink like I asked you to?"

"Of course," he quickly replied. He poured Gabriana a double shot of the cognac and told her it was on him.

As Gabriana emptied the glass, she began to relax a little. Swigging the last gulp, she pushed her glass forward and looked up at the flat-screen plasma television mounted above the bar. That's when the special report bulletin cut the local news broadcast short.

"HIP-HOP SENSATION, KEON 'SCHOLAR' JAMISON, WAS SHOT AND KILLED."

....

"Police are saying..."....

Gabriana was hearing, but she was no longer listening. Instantly, nausea took over.

"Wake up, Gabriana," she whispered to herself. "Wake up, right now." With her eyes glued upward on the screen, she saw nothing but black-and-purple balls of light. She felt down with her right hand and found her left one. She began pinching and pinching, chanting aloud, "Wake up, wake up. Gabriana, please wake up, please wake up."

Gabriana never woke up that evening. *This was real and it was too late.*

Part II

Chapter 13

11:37 pm New Year's Eve

Gabriana lay on her stomach, across the bed, trying her best to conclude the long email. So much had happened and there was so much to say. Cracking her fingers a few times, she continued to type.

I laid there paralyzed. The cramps were horrible, but my thoughts were worse. The nurses had left me alone and I couldn't stop thinking, or crying. I thought about the last text that I had received from Scholar the night before I flew out to Miami to be with him. I remembered how he told me in those simple text message words, "Luv you my lady." I never got to tell him how much I loved him back after that. I mean, there were so many distractions from the moment I boarded the plane, I just never got to tell him. I thought about that horrible realization over and over as I continued to lay on that hard hospital bed, crying and cramping. I thought about our fight and how I told him I hated him, and never wanted to see him again, then I remembered the last time we both looked at each other and what I saw on his face that night. It was crazy. What I saw? I saw the innocence of every human soul. Whew! When I say that I saw the guilt, the pain, the fear and the confusion of that one human soul, sitting right there in front of me, that is exactly what I saw on his face as we stared at each other. Lying there months later, I regretted so much. With what I saw going on inside of Scholar that night, I thought about how I did not stop him from leaving that room. I did not comfort him in his ultimate distress. They say when a person who never breaks down, breaks down, they really break down. I witnessed this firsthand, but did nothing. I watched my dude lose it. I mean, straight up lose it, and I didn't question him as to why. I just looked at him. I was too angry. He needed me so bad at that moment that he could not even express the emotion in words, so he cried. Wow, I cried out so loud thinking about this in that room that the nurses came rushing to my side. Then they wheeled me into surgery. As I slept through the operation, I dreamed of Mama. Then I woke up anxious, so the nurses sedated me some more. Once I was calmed, I asked one of the nurses if I could hold her. She obliged and left the room. I knew what had happened, but still it had to be confirmed. So the nurse returned with an older nurse by her side. She was a very soothing nurse, she comforted me. I held my arms out to embrace my first-born daughter, Scholar's first-born daughter. I named her Skylar Keona Jamison. Her body was so frail. She had been through everything that her mommy had endured. I kissed her cheek. Her lifeless body was so unreal to me. Man, I do not know how I walked out of that hospital a few days later. I mean walking out of there all alone? But like Mama used to say to me, "The peace of GOD surpasses all understanding." It was either that or I was totally numb. Well, the next day, my baby was properly laid to rest, right there next to her dad. This was thanks to Scholar's family. Yep, I am glad the latter year is over. I lost so much in such a small amount of time. I'm still coping. Like I said in the beginning of this email, I miss you dearly. And I am hoping that you will return your friendship to me. It's been a minute friend, but please come back. I Love You, Khali, forever - Gabriana! ~

Gabriana then pressed *Send*.

12:00am.

Gabriana put the fire to the blunt. She pushed the huge peach pillows up against the wall, then placed her back to their cushion. "Happy New Year! Let's hope," she said to herself as she exhaled the thick smoke. Gabriana began to drift. Before she closed her eyes, she said a final goodbye to Scholar and Skylar. "Happy New Year, Mama, I hope you get better," she added.

Janette's illness had taken a turn for the worse after Scholar was killed. Already in poor condition, she had to literally get on a plane to go get her daughter. Gabriana never boarded her flight that dreadful night. Instead, she took a trip to one of Miami's finest ERs at the local hospital. Right now to this day, Gabriana couldn't tell anybody what happened after she heard that news broadcast. She completely blanked out. The anxiety attack was so severe that she had to be sedated into a deep slumber. Once back home, the chaos was unbelievable. Scholar's family was all over the news, pleading for any leads on the whereabouts of those people still pending arrest for his murder. His bodyguard, Jason, was not cooperating completely with the investigators. He was behaving like a madman. To Gabriana, that made him appear suspicious. Once the reward was offered, it didn't take long for the police to get a story, the names and whereabouts of the culprits involved.

The official explanation given to the family was this:

Scholar had earned a few foes while spending time out in Miami. There were supposedly some local cats who had been scoping Scholar for a minute. Everyone called one of them Jude, and the other one, Scorch. Word was they had it out for Scholar because of his mouth. Jude was a younger cousin of Brick's and also one of his Miami-based goons. That Friday, before his death, Scholar had spent the night out on the town with Jason. The bodyguard was also a local Miami native himself. Scholar had been staying at Jason's condo since the fight with Gabriana on Thursday night. One witness, Neceive Bradford, told the officials that on Friday night, while Scholar, Jason and a few other fellas sat and talked in the downstairs lounge of a strip bar, Brick and Jude came down to hangout. According to the story that Neceive gave the police, Brick and Scholar got into a shouting match. There were a lot of disagreements going on between the duo and the tension had been thick for weeks. But that night, the two former friends really came to blows and it all got crazy from there. "Those niggas were throwing drinks and money at each

125

other, and everything. It got real nasty." He went on to tell how Brick wouldn't calm down, so he ended up receiving a thorough beat down by Jason. "It took about five or six niggas to get Jason off that man." Neceive confirmed that after that incident, all night Brick called Scholar's phone, threatening him. Saturday evening, as Scholar returned to Jason's building, Jude and the assailant, Scorch, confronted him before he could reach the entrance. They tried to rob Scholar, but he didn't have much on him, except for two cell phones. While the two goons were taking the phones and what little cash Scholar had on him, Jason came out of the apartment building, blasting on sight. When Jude hit the ground, his partner took off running. When the bodyguard turned to chase, instead of shooting the guy with the gun in his hand, Brick's dying cousin shot the one closest to him.

Scholar died before the ambulance arrived. He suffered a fatal gunshot wound to the chest.

Kevin "Brick" Degrassi, was later arrested and charged with second degree murder. Since he and Scholar were no longer teammates, Brick had supposedly orchestrated the hit.

Gabriana only bit part of that story. Some things just didn't quite add up for her. For one, why had Brick screamed at the news reporters. He was cuffed up, but continued to yell out, "I didn't do nothing. I'm being setup. Scholar was set up. He was set up and so was I." That was something to be considered. Then there was the police report. Scholar was reportedly killed around 6:30pm. But he had left Gabriana at about 1:00pm. So where was he for the five unaccounted hours before he arrived at Jason's? No one knew. Where was his gun? And where was his jewelry? Gabriana told the detectives that Scholar was wearing a $65,000 diamond encrusted watch, and a diamond earring stud the last time she saw him. She always observed him closely. So where were the diamond pieces? Nobody had an answer for that either. There was no jewelry whatsoever found on the bodies. Only the two cell phones and a little cash were found on Jude. But Gabriana insisted that there should have been three phones on Scholar. He always carried two of his own, plus he had her phone. Jason told the detectives that perhaps the runaway assailant had the jewel pieces; and as far as a missing cellular phone goes, he knew nothing about that.

Everyone suspected that Scorch was this unknown person of interest. But Scorch was in the wind and there was no trail left behind for the police to follow. Therefore, he was never apprehended for questioning on the murder or the stolen items. Scorch simply disappeared.

Another thing that bothered Gabriana were the condos where Jason resided. The stretched-out units were not only on private property, but the buildings, and their surrounding acres were all under construction. So there weren't any additional witnesses to confirm Jason's account of what had happened. Mainly, there was only this Neceive character to coincide with Jason's interrogation. Gabriana had never heard of that nigga in her life. Scholar never mentioned the name to her. That name was unique, how could she forget it if they were ever introduced? Gabriana couldn't stop wondering things. *Jason is a trained killer. How is it that the other assailant ran off? And where is this Scorch guy anyway?* Everything going on was sideways. Nothing made sense and Gabriana hoped the officials felt the same. The investigation should be drawn out. There were some missing pieces to the puzzle that needed to be picked up. Gabriana thought about this until her head spun. She wanted to do something to avenge Scholar, or bring him real justice, but she was useless, and she felt pretty lost.

Jason was a licensed professional security guard and he was hired to kill. Scholar had informed Gabriana about that as soon as he brought him around. Unfortunately, Gabriana didn't get to spend enough time with the guard to personally get to know him for herself.

Jason was never charged with shooting and killing Jude. After it was all over with, Jason moved to Los Angeles. However, Scholar's other top guard, Bear, continued to keep in touch with Gabriana. He told her about his own suspicions regarding everything that went down. "My vibe is off with this whole situation. I'm going to get to the bottom of this. Scholar was like family to me. I'm never letting off 'til I get peace...and I don't have no peace," he cried to Gabriana.

Gabriana understood and agreed. She too would avenge her man's death, but the time would have to be right, and she would have to be very slick about it. That was fine by her, but Gabriana knew that in order to be very calculating and thorough, she would have to one day get her mind right. But who knew how long that could take?

Chapter 14

On Valentine's day, Gabriana received a call from Khali. She was so excited to finally hear from him. They talked for about an hour over the phone. Khali knew about Gabriana's initial lost, but he had no idea that she had been pregnant. After reading her email, he wondered how far along she was at the time of her delivery. *If she was anywhere near a seven-month mark, then there's a good chance...*"

Gabriana and Khali had spent many nights together while Scholar was away. Only twice had they truly crossed the line during those many nights at different hotels. Even so, somewhere in the back of Khali's mind, he wondered if the deceased baby girl was his. Their encounters had been so unexpected that each time they had been irresponsible on every level. They never used protection. Both Gabriana and Khali knew there was a possibility of conception. It was always their little secret.

Gabriana expressed to Khali how much she wanted to see him. He consented and she gave him the directions to where she was staying. Gabriana had purchased a condo thanks to an account Scholar had started for her. She moved swiftly, preparing herself and her living environment for Khali's arrival. Gabriana had been really lonely lately. With no more Scholar, Toree, Milan and Ciona around, she spent all of her time alone. Time to time she would visit with Jannette, but it was always a mental setback for Gabriana. She could feel something in the air whenever she sat around her mother too long. Also, she had not forgotten what she saw through that window the night she dreamed that fateful dream.

The first thing Khali noticed when he walked into the spacious living room was Gabriana's hair. She had cut the length to fall just above her shoulders, and she wore it curly again. She was more than beautiful in his eyes. Khali was almost in a trance, looking upon her.

"Are you just going to stare at me or are you going to say something?" she asked with a chuckle.

Before he could get his words out, Gabriana hugged him and wouldn't let go. It took a few seconds, but Khali returned the hug with tight arms. So many thoughts rushed through both of their minds.

Gabriana and Khali laid parallel to each other, across her bed, and talked. It was just like they used to do in those hotel rooms. The only change was the stories. Gabriana expressed to Khali how lonely she had been lately, and Khali revealed that he also had been spending much time alone.

"You were always sort of a loner, Khali," Gabriana teased.

"True, but the difference is then it was optional, now it's like I don't really trust or like people, so it's like I'm forced to ride solo, you feel me?"

Gabriana thought about Scholar's similar words. She quickly shook it off. "Why? What are you talking about?" she asked, turning her eyes from the ceiling to face him.

"I don't know and I can't really explain it. It's just a restless feeling that's been over me for a minute now. I mean, I ain't out here playing in dirt," Khali quickly added. "But no matter what it is I'm doing, I feel uneasy, fo'real." He shook his head. "And then, I'm up at all times of night. You know why? Because when I sleep, I see things and when I'm awake, guess what, I still see things."

The room became still.

Gabriana inquired, "Do you still have that book that you used to write in all the time, Khali?"

"I have a *few* of those books."

"Can I see them?"

He looked over into her eyes. "You already *see them.*"

As Gabriana returned Khali's gaze, she caught chill bumps and sat up in the bed. "Khali, tell me what the hell you are talking about," she said in stern, shaky voice.

Khali ran his tongue across his upper teeth, but did not speak. He thought about the contents he had written in those books. Also, he thought of the dreams, the revelations and the coincidences. He wanted to share it all with Gabriana, but he was unsure if the time was right. So, the only response he offered was, "Gabriana, do you have dreams?"

This was the first time he had ever asked her that question. The two of them had discussed many things, except dreams.

A shocked Gabriana opened and closed her mouth. She had never mentioned her dreams to Khali. To her, Scholar had trained her to keep them locked away inside. Seizing the opportunity to discuss them with someone, she nodded.

Khali reached his hand over and squeezed hers. "Tell me," he gently said.

"I don't know. I don't want you to perceive me in that light."

"In what light?" Khali was now anticipating her honesty.

"I don't want you to think I'm crazy-weird or something," she said, biting down on her bottom lip. *Another trait she had picked up from*

131

Khali frowned, and then relaxed his face. "Listen, it doesn't matter how someone perceives you. Say what's on your mind anyway. You'll either make the connection or you won't." He advised.

Gabriana contemplated his words. She removed her hand from Khali's then placed both of her hands over her face. "Ughh," was all she let out.

Khali reached over again, removing her hands from her face. He then pulled her backward and rolled over. Shifting his weight onto his side, he placed his mouth near her ear. Slowly and carefully he whispered, "If you tell me about yours, I'll tell you about mine."

Just then, Gabriana's phone started ringing with Scholar's ringtone blaring. This made her jump and turn her attention toward the direction of the phone. Khali cursed inside. Gabriana tried to sit up, but he pulled her back down. "No, I need to answer that," she said, trying to escape his hold. As Gabriana removed herself from the bed to check the phone, she felt Khali's eyes on her.

Gabriana walked over to her phone and connected the call.

"Hello?"

"Hey, girl. Happy Valentine's Day. How have you been holding up, Gabriana?" Milan asked.

Pause

"Good," was all a stunned Gabriana could reply.

"Are you sure about that?" Ciona intercepted.

Gabriana's reply was a simple word. *"Wow."*

Chapter 15

Four months had passed since Gabriana's closest friends came back into her life. Khali, Milan and Ciona were hanging tough and the three couldn't have returned at a better time. Gabriana really did need them in her life. The way her mother had been sick all the time was taking its toll on her.

Gabriana stood on her mother's back porch, smoking and thinking. She thought of Jannette and Khali. *Why is it that she could never accept Scholar, but she seems to take to Khali so well?* From the very moment that Gabriana introduced the two, they smiled and greeted each other like they had history. It was like the both of them were harboring a secret. Gabriana could not figure it out. "'That's crazy," she said as she tossed the cigarette butt into the grass. She then entered the backdoor.

Khali stayed inside the living room, talking with Jannette. After another week under observation, Janette had only been discharged from the hospital for two hours. Gabriana and Khali were awaiting her every need.

Gabriana returned to the stovetop counter and removed the lid from the pot. She wasn't much of a cook, but if her mama wanted spaghetti, then spaghetti it would be. Jannette had not been eating much and was losing a substantial amount of weight. As a result of that, Gabriana was also dropping pounds. Life was always killing Gabriana's appetite, so she rarely ate. To maintain life, Gabriana nibbled on fruit, drank a lot of water, and on the days when she just could not eat, she would drink Ensure protein beverages. She was already, slightly taller and thinner than average, but now with the excess weight dissolving, Gabriana could easily have impressed any model recruiter. However, this caused concern amongst those who actually cared about her health.

Jannette and Khali entered the kitchen.

"Is it ready yet? I'm starving," a weak Jannette said. She took a seat at the table. So did Khali.

"Indeed, hungry monsters," Gabriana joked as she added the final herbs to the thick sauce. After compiling the sauce, meat and noodles, she fixed both Jannette and Khali large plates and handed them bottled water. She then grabbed an apple from the bowl on the kitchen counter and took a seat at the table.

Both Jannette and Khali looked up at Gabriana like she was crazy.

"Eat," they both said in unison.

"Okay," Gabriana replied defeated. She got up to fix herself a tiny plate.

The three of them sat and had a quiet lunch together. Jannette broke the silence.

"I want the two of you to come to church with me in the morning," she stated.

Gabriana didn't reply. She just sighed and continued to pick at the noodles on her full plate.

"Not a problem, we will be there," Khali assured her with a slight smirk on his face.

Gabriana rolled her eyes at both Khali and Jannette. *I should take my dang on food back*, she thought. But her face said it all out loud.

The following morning, Gabriana, Khali and Jannette sat in the third row from the front in the church. They were facing the pulpit. The preacher was a short, older man with gray eyes. His eyes were very piercing and made Gabriana uncomfortable, so she glanced over and around him. *Why the hell is he looking at me,* her conscious said to her.

Pastor Hill spoke with fire and conviction in his voice as he delivered the sermon. Gabriana wanted to block out his words, but could not. He was preaching about people having callings on their lives. "You can run, but you cannot hide," he said. "You are held accountable for the responsibilities required of your life." Gabriana tried to endure the service, but the last straw was when Pastor Hill began to lecture to the congregation about not following those callings and the result of sin being death. Gabriana's mind roamed to Scholar and his death. Then she started meditating on her own death. Suddenly, the room was spinning. Gabriana's temperature rose rapidly, but she trembled as if she were cold. She tried to calm her heaving chest with breathing exercises. It didn't work. When Gabriana glanced to her right to look at Khali, she noticed the tears that he could not wipe away fast enough. His knees were bouncing up and down at a rapid pace. Gabriana's ears filled with an unknown liquid and her body felt like it was sinking into the wood bench she was seated on.

"*I got to get out of here,*" she mumbled to herself. Gabriana tried to stand, but she felt glued to the seat. She scratched her thighs with her nails. She then glanced down at the inside of her wrist and snapped. *This was a mistake, I should not have come here.*

The thoughts would not cease. Finally able to stand, Gabriana excused herself and walked briskly down the center aisle toward the door. She couldn't get there fast enough. She was almost running, and she could feel the eyes on her, but she didn't care. At that moment, Gabriana wished that she could fly. "This is too much playing," she said aloud once she finally made it outside.

Gabriana got into her BMW and sped off as fast as she could. The loud screeching could be heard inside the church. She didn't care that Jannette and Khali had rode with her. They would just have to find their own way home or ride that church bus.

She was out of there.

~ ~ ~

That night, while Gabriana lay awake in her bed, she reminisced about Scholar's funeral.

There was a lot of media coverage and so many people everywhere. Gabriana sat alone in the BMW with the doors locked. Her mother stood outside of the driver's side, banging on the window. Gabriana couldn't hear her. She just sat there, sobbing like an injured child. The only person who could get Gabriana out of that car was Tina, Scholar's mother.

The woman was a "boss." Tina marched right over to that car. Using the extra set of keys that Gabriana had given her, she hit the unlock sensor and snatched Gabriana out. "Woman up! He's gone," was the only thing Tina said before hugging her. Then she broke down herself.

Gabriana remembered approaching the casket.

She didn't know whose arm was wrapped around her shoulders as she slowly approached Scholar. Gabriana felt so lost and confused. She stood there, looking up at the ceiling before finally forcing herself to look down. She had not had the strength or will to make it out of the car the night before for Scholar's wake. Now at the funeral, Gabriana stood face-to-face with the most powerless situation she had ever dealt with.

It was definitely her boyfriend. Scholar was laid out beautifully in his final resting bed. He was one of the few people who actually didn't look

138

dead. He looked like he was sleeping. Scholar's face was a little swollen, but for the most part, he looked like himself and this made it worse for his mourners. Gabriana glanced down at his folded hands. That's when she saw the flaw.

Blood.

There were small traces of blood under the tips of his fingers. Fluid rushed to the top of Gabriana's head. Unconsciously, she bent her face down toward his. She felt the hands on her back and some on her arms. Gabriana didn't care. She moved in close to her man and gently kissed his nose. The skin that was once so warm with life was now cold. The scent of the cologne that she loved so much was no longer there. Instead, it was replaced with another smell, the sickening stench of death. There was no more "I AM KING." Only "I AM DEAD" lingered. She thought she would be able to kiss his lips, too, but the first touch ended it all. Stained in vomit, Gabriana was rushed to the nearest emergency room. She felt poisoned.

The ringing phone interrupted Gabriana's horrible memories. She answered on the first ring. It was Khali.

"Hi," she greeted him. The call was on time and more than welcomed.

Khali responded dryly, "Yo, what up?"

The first ten minutes of their conversation was nothing more than Gabriana's small talk. Khali was acting weird. Becoming irritated, she asked, "Okay, what is wrong with you, Khali? Are you upset because I left you and Mama hanging earlier?"

After a long pause, Khali said, "I did it. I walked down the aisle and turned my life over."

His voice was strained.

At first, Gabriana didn't reply 'cause it took her a good minute to understand what he was talking about. Once it registered she finally spoke. "So what are you saying, Khali? You are tripping right now."

"Nah. No, I'm not. I'm a changed man, Gabriana. I did it, and now I have to be on point, fo'real. I mean, I don't know what's next, but I'm letting a lot of things go."

Gabriana breathed dragon air.

"Even me, nigga? Huh, even me? So you're about to become another Mama on me? Or are you leaving me behind?" she asked with a sarcastic-laced attitude.

Khali held his response for a moment. When he did speak, he simply said, "I don't know. All know is it was time to wake up. I needed to—"

Click

Gabriana hung up the phone. She had heard enough and she was furious. "So you just going to take another person from me? Just like that, right? You know what, just like you obviously don't like me, I don't like you either," she coldly said aloud. Gabriana was angry with God, and for the first time in many months, she cried herself to sleep. She felt like she had suffered another loss.

Chapter 16

It had been a whole week since Gabriana had that conversation with Khali. He called her several times, but she would not answer or return his calls and texts. When Khali would come by, he would end up spending his time with Jannette because Gabriana wasn't dealing with him. She would act as if he wasn't there or leave when he arrived. The pitiful look in his round eyes pleaded his case, but she ignored him.

Gabriana spent the following two weeks strictly hanging around Ciona and Milan. When she was finally ready to talk to Khali again, she couldn't get in touch with him. He had stopped coming by, and when she called and sent him text messages, he wouldn't reply. *Ugh!*

One evening, Gabriana overheard Jannette speaking with Khali on the phone, so she eavesdropped. Overhearing the end of the conversation, Gabriana learned that Khali was still attending open mics. Putting the pieces together, she now knew where she could catch up with him. She just had to put her plan together and execute it.

Monday night, Gabriana and Milan headed to Lights. They arrived late because it took Gabriana a while to get dressed. She wanted to look especially good that night. For some reason, Gabriana felt she had to compete for Khali's attention.

But who am I competing with, God?

The audience cheered as Khali exited the stage. *Here we go,* Gabriana thought.

She watched Khali head over to the bar and order a soda. This was her opportunity. Gabriana told Milan to go to the opposite end of the bar and order her two shots of Patron. She handed her the money and watched as Milan walked away. Gabriana slipped into the restroom to adjust her makeup. She stayed in there until she was certain she was ready. When Gabriana exited the restroom, she spotted Milan at a small table with the drinks. She headed over. Never taking a seat or saying a word, Gabriana downed both shots and headed toward Khali.

To say the conversation went bad would have been an understatement. Although Gabriana's intentions were to have a cool conversation and straighten things out with Khali, things went south. He did not give Gabriana the attention she hoped for. She saw no look of admiration on his face when he looked on her.

"Khali, what's up baby? Where you been hiding?

"I've been chilling."

"Yeah, well, what's been going on? Are you upset with me about something?"

"Nah."

"I can't tell."

"I'm straight."

For every question she asked him, there were only nonchalant answers returned. No details and no emotion. In fact, another female who walked over to Khali to compliment his performance, received more love than her. After this went on for so long, Gabriana snapped on him.

"You know what? You are so fake, dude. You know what, fu—"

"Don't curse at me, Gabriana," Khali interrupted.

"I do what I want to do and that's the problem, huh? You can't handle me. You can't even handle yourself, so you're running, how weak is that? You're lame." Gabriana stressed her disdain through squinted eyes.

Being new to his conversion, Khali had not mastered the "peace of God" yet, so he snapped back. Soon, the argument escalated.

"Huh? Hold on, you need to watch ya mouth, fo'real."

"I can't stand a nigga like you. I don't need to watch nothing but *you*. You just a fake—"

"Fake? Gabriana, you need to step off 'cuz you're coming off like a real knucklehead right now. You can't ever in your life use that term on me. You're the phoniest person on the planet. Get lost! I'm not hearing nothing you have to say right now." Khali grabbed Gabriana's arm and shoved her away from him.

"Don't touch me, Khali! Make me get lost," she taunted. "You don't own—"

"You are whack, Gabriana! Why would you want to talk to someone who doesn't want you around? I said get away from me."

Khali tried to grab her arm again, but Gabriana snatched it away and pushed him. "I said don't touch me."

Now she was ready to clown. Gabriana was never the chick to act up in public. She wasn't into making a spectacle of herself in front of an audience for no one, unless it was truly necessary.

And it was necessary.

"Yo, Milan, get this chick away from me." Khali widened his eyes at Milan who was approaching. "Yo, step off. I'm not playing," he warned, looking back at Gabriana.

"No."

"You are embarrassing yourself. You always on some clown sh…" Khali caught himself before he cursed. "Gabriana, I'm not that dude. Step off. You're used to these cowboys around here. I'm not one of 'em, word up. You have the mind of a child. I don't see why I ever bothered with you. You wanna front on *me* when you have been nothing but fake when it comes to ME. Real doesn't live in you. Yo, you're selfish. You think you gonna just use me when you feel the need. Nah, this is my world and I don't want a little girl like you in it. Point blank. Shake!"

People were now watching. Khali was going off. He went on and on, telling Gabriana how messed up of a person he felt she was. Before he realized it, he brought up Scholar's name. "If that nigga Scholar was around, you wouldn't be bothered with me. You've always been twisted around that nigga's nuts. Yo, don't play me."

"That's not true."

"It's absolutely true. The only reason I stuck around you is 'cuz I know how lost you are. It's never been about me."

"That's a lie and you know it! Stop lying, Khali," Gabriana screamed in his face.

Khali felt the only reason Gabriana came back for him was because she was lonely without Scholar. Until now, he had never mentioned how he really felt. So at the moment's opportunity, Khali expressed those very feelings to Gabriana.

"I'm tired of you. You don't know a nigga like me. All you know is puppet niggas with coins in their pockets. That nigga Scholar deleted mad brain cells from your head! You think that nigga had your heart, but I say he had your mind. He didn't care about your feelings, not fo'real. It's mad chicks that got down with him. For some strange reason, you think that nigga made you somebody. You just another little freak. Get out of here! You're nothing because you don't know who you are."

Gabriana couldn't believe her ears. Her thoughts ran wild because she wanted to thoroughly check Khali for being a hypocrite. Gabriana scolded him inside her mind. *If you are so concerned about all the women that Scholar had sex with, then maybe you should have taken precautions when you was screwing me, nigga. Whatever diseases I dodged, you also dodged too, fool!* She wanted to bust Khali out loud; point out that they all could have got AIDS. Everyone involved played the deadly game of Russian roulette with their poor decisions. But she wouldn't dare expose them like that. Not in front of strangers, so she took another approach. Gabriana started screaming obscenities on Khali because she was embarrassed. Milan tried to tell her to walk away but she wouldn't listen. She knew the root of all this bull Khali was giving her and she wasn't having it. "You are a HATER! My man is gone and look at you…you're still jealous. Grow up!"

"You sound stupid. Why would I be jealous of someone who's *DEAD?*" Khali put emphasis on that last word to rub it in. He wanted to hurt Gabriana because he really *was* jealous.

Gabriana froze in place. She watched Khali as he said, "Let the dead be dead! Get over it!"

Ironically, the phone in Gabriana's hand started blaring Scholar's ringtone. Khali snapped and smacked it out of her hand. It flew to the floor and broke into pieces.

Before Gabriana could react, Khali said, "Even from beyond the grave this nigga's blocking. Can somebody call the Ghostbusters, *please*?!"

Gabriana had heard enough. She slapped *fire* onto Khali's face. The wrath of her palm brought Khali back down to earth.

As Milan pulled her backward, Gabriana yelled, "Don't ever disrespect him!...Ever!" Her face swelled up with the excruciating suffering that she had hidden so well until now. Khali had never witnessed that from her. He regretted his words right away, but it was too late to take them back.

"That was *evil*," she continued. "Don't *ever* do that again. Ever!" Gabriana then spat a bullet of spit on Khali and walked away. Those standing around, watching, did not hesitate to move out of her path. She was a walking flame.

"*I got you, baby,*" she said to Scholar in her heart. Gabriana remembered that all he wanted was his respect.

~ ~ ~

Late that night, Gabriana laid restlessly in her bed, channel surfing when she heard someone lightly knocking at the front door. At first, she thought she was hearing things, but then the tapping sounded again. She went to the door and looked through the peephole. It was Khali.

Gabriana had already learned the ultimate lesson of turning her back on someone whom she loved out of anger from her final encounter with Scholar. Not wanting to make that mistake again, she didn't hesitate to let Khali inside. Gabriana didn't look at him as he entered the doorway, she just headed back to bed.

146

Initially, she was waiting for Khali to come into her room, but he didn't, so she dozed off. Gabriana was unaware that Khali had gone into her bathroom to pray. Almost a full hour later, she felt the cover lift as he slipped into her bed. Gabriana shifted and reached for the remote. She turned the television off and then turned to face Khali. His eyes were fixed upward. She knew he probably wanted to talk it out, but Gabriana had a point to prove. So she moved in.

First, she kissed his neck gently. There were no words exchanged as she repeatedly placed her lips on his neck. Then she skillfully took his earlobe into her mouth. Khali blinked a few times, but never turned his eyes from the ceiling. Gabriana placed one hand on his chest and moved in closer until she was on top of him. Kissing him on his lips, she looked into his eyes. She had his full attention. Gabriana began kissing his neck again. She could feel his heartbeat speed up as his chest heaved up and down. When she took one of his hands, and slowly placed it on her inner thigh, he began to lose his breath. As soon as he began to massage the flesh of that area, she knew she had him. Khali tried to speak, but the seductress hushed him with her mouth. With focused eyes, she pulled back, and ordered, "Shhhh, no talking." Gabriana sat up on Khali, and like an expert, she placed one of the fingers of his other hand into her mouth. She intentionally began the art of seduction, and it worked like good technology.

Once Gabriana got her way, she put it on poor Khali as if it was his last night on planet Earth. His body was putty when it came to the female he was in love with. He never could maintain control.

Satisfied with her accomplishment, Gabriana closed her eyes, in hopes of falling sleep. Before she drifted completely, she smiled within. *Ha, you wasn't just thinking about your God when we just got it on. Converted, huh? Yeah, sure, this nigga is fooling himself.*

147

~ ~ ~

It was almost 5:00 in the morning. Khali just laid there next to Gabriana. His eyes were red and he was hurt because he felt weak. He wiped off the single tear that escaped his eye. He had never been a weak nigga, so he didn't understand why he felt so weak now. It hurt badly and he felt guilt and shame.

As a young boy, Khali's grandfather used to take him out to the country. His grandfather owned some property near a lake. Beautiful trees surrounded the property. Every weekend, he would take Khali out to help him build a cabin house. His grandfather had been singlehandedly building that cabin for years. Some weekends, he would have a couple of his buddies assist him with the harder parts of the job, but it was his vision alone that they worked off of. Khali's father had been killed in a terrible motorcycle accident when the boy was only three years old. Immediately, the grandfather took over the responsibility of raising the boy into a man. During those trips to work on the cabin house, Khali's grandfather would chop wood into hug logs and have an eight-year-old Khali carry the loads around the property. At first, Khali would cry and complain, but eventually his strength grew. His grandfather did not care about any of the tears or whining. He would tell Khali that what didn't kill him would only make him stronger. Khali, being so young, would reply with questions, such as, "Why do I have to be strong when I feel weak?" Every time he said something like that, his grandfather would gently shove him to the ground. One day, Khali had asked him why he always shoved him to the ground. His grandfather looked the little boy right in the eyes and told him something that he would never forget. He said, "Because boy, the only time a man is weak is when he is lying down, remember that."

Khali chuckled a little when he recalled that memory. He then repositioned his body from the lying position to that of one sitting up. He removed the pillow and tossed it to the floor. Then he placed his back to

148

the cool wall and rubbed his low hair with both hands. Khali inhaled a deep breath then released the air in the form of a long sigh. He looked over at Gabriana, then lowered his hands from his head. He gently lifted the cover from her body and examined her. She was peacefully lying on her side. He rolled her over onto her back. Gabriana stirred a little, but did not wake up. He looked down at her, and continued to study her in silence. Khali reviewed the deep scar that tarnished the otherwise smooth skin on her stomach. *That must be a result of the surgery for the baby.* Next, Khali studied the permanent scars on Gabriana's dark-brown face. There were not many, only two. The first one was a slightly dented abrasion just below the left side of her hairline. The other scar was a small but deep dark line located on her left cheek. No one really noticed this scar because Gabriana's dimples caught all the attention. Khali was unaware that those war wounds on her face were the result of her last fight with Scholar. What Khali *did* understand were the marks on the inside of Gabriana's right wrist. Although very thin, there were many of those line-like slashes. They were clearly the result of a razor.

Khali left the bed and reapplied his clothes. He stood over Gabriana for a few minutes, watching her.

He then whispered, "She's still shuffling the cards…she's not ready to deal."

With bloodshot eyes, Khali walked out of Gabriana's bedroom, her apartment, and her life.

Chapter 17

Gabriana was tired of buying new phones. "This is some bull," she said as she exited the cellular store. Back at her apartment, she plugged the new phone into the charger. The battery would need to charge for at least two hours if Gabriana didn't want to get caught out there. Trying to kill some time in-between, she decided to do some cleaning. Gabriana plugged her iPod into the computer and got busy. Once the hard parts of the condo were cleaned, she went through the overstuffed drawers that she never had time to organize.

Going through the last drawer, Gabriana made the discovery.

She stared down at the disconnected Sidekick phone. The police had retrieved it from the body of Brick's cousin and returned it to Tina. In return, Tina had given it back to Gabriana as they entered the church for Scholar's funeral. After her boyfriend was officially placed in the ground, a distraught Gabriana had tossed the phone in a drawer.

Gabriana immediately went through her drawer of old chargers and retrieved what she was searching for. Twenty minutes later, she returned to the slightly charged Sidekick. She lay backward on the bed as she opened it.

After a few short minutes of searching and reading, Gabriana's eyes set fixed on the screen. "No," she said hardly audible. "No."

Gabriana could not believe what she had just read inside the files of her text messages.

…....

9:55pm

FWD:

See da msg below nigga and undrstnd tht I'm not play'n...I'm going 2 ask u ths 1time only..who r U and state your bisness wit my wife!

———————————

~ Baby, pls give me a call. I need 2 talk to u asap! If you can, pls, I want to come over...wherever you are, I want to come. ~

———————————

9:57pm

FWD: RE:

First of all, she ain't your wife, nigga...2nd...Why dnt u ask HER who I am... Stay on ur job and u wn't have 2 do your homework later. And if u want to know if I smashed your girl...the answer is yes! No joke, it was pretty good 2..and it got better every time i hit...now take that how u want! ~ King Khali

———————————

9:59pm

FWD: RE: RE:

Fo'real nigga...u getn it in ...thts ur answer?!! Is it really like tht...she been up undr u b'hind my back right?! OK... thts cool...but keep ur vest on fam cuz i'm putn a bullet in u when I find out who u r!

———————————

10:01pm

FWD: RE: RE: RE:

Ohhhhh...this getn interest'n! LoL nigga!.. wow u real emotional rght now but if I were u I wld be really upset 2 ;)... tell Gabri I said wassup! - King Khali

…...

Gabriana was shocked and hurt. She couldn't believe Khali!

That night when Scholar went crazy on her, it was because Khali had thrown gasoline on an already-blazing fire. Those text messages were exchanged only minutes before she had arrived back at Scholar's room.

That's why he was trying to kill me, 'cause of this nigga!

Scholar had went through Gabriana's phone while she was out. She knew now that he had probably read many more of the messages that were sent back and forth between her and Khali. That revelation stung Gabriana's heart like a billion honeybees. She realized how much that must have hurt Scholar, and that's what sent him over the edge that awful night.

Gabriana tried to call Khali at least twenty times in a row, but got no answer.

"What is wrong with you, Khali?!" she screamed.

Gabriana stood in her room in a state of fury. The tears falling from her eyes felt like they were boiling. With one mighty swoop of the arm, Gabriana knocked everything from atop her dresser. Makeup, books and a picture all came crashing down onto the floor. She looked down at the picture of her and Scholar hugged up in L.A. The picture of the couple was beautiful and the love displayed on it looked so genuine. Gabriana took a seat next to the broken glass. She placed her hand on top of Scholar's face then felt the sting of a cut. Picking the small fragments of glass from the palm of her hand, Gabriana then set her attention on the marks inside of her wrist. Covering the wrist with her other hand, she began to rock back and forth as the memories returned.

She remembered lying on the bathroom floor. The pregnancy test laid next to her balled up body. The floor all around her was slippery with tears, saliva and vomit. She gathered the energy to get on her hands and knees. She crawled over to the door and locked it. She had been staying at Jannette's house, and did not want her to enter and try to stop what was about to happen. Next, she crawled over to the cabinet located beneath the sink. Moving at an animated pace, she pulled the small vanity basket from the cabinet and removed the sharp razor blade. She began with light sweeps, but the harder the tears fell, the harder the razor dug into her soft skin. The razor's edge finally made its way to the vein and the blood began to leak, then pour. Gabriana laid her weak body in the warm blood and closed her eyes. She never heard her mother break the door in. She never heard the EMT staff. She didn't hear anything for two days.

Looking back, prior to the actual confirmation from the test, Gabriana had an idea that she was pregnant all along. Instead of taking new precautions, she continued to do things in the same manner as before the suspicion had arrived. As a matter of fact, she blocked the suspicion all together. She acted as if there were no changes within her body, period. She wasn't ready to deal with that.

The reality of it all hit her the seventh week after Scholar was killed. That was why she had decided to take the test. The results showed up positive on the little white stick. Fortunately, Gabriana's suicide attempt did not terminate her pregnancy. The bigger her stomach grew, the more she felt her sanity return. This was during the daylight hours. During the nights, Gabriana cried. She hated with all her heart that Scholar was not around to see his first-born. When Gabriana learned that the child she was carrying was a girl, she was ecstatic. She did not want a boy. Gabriana felt that there were already too many black boys without their fathers. She did not want her son to be a part of that statistic. She felt more confident that she could do the job of raising her little girl alone. True, little girls need their fathers, but Gabriana wasn't thinking straight. She was only coping. She read and talked to her daughter every day. She even composed songs to sing to the unborn baby. Gabriana was so excited to meet her. She gave her so much private attention, love and affection, constantly, until the day the cramps came.

Chapter 18

Another week passed. Gabriana did not know if she was more upset about the foul text messages that Khali had sent to Scholar or the fact that she had not heard from him. Needing to get out, Gabriana called her girls.

By 7:00pm., Gabriana, Ciona and Milan were out enjoying a late happy hour. Feeling her drinks, Gabriana couldn't help but think of Khali. She wanted to talk to him, so she decided to send him a text. It read:

_____

~ Ha, nigga u sho'rght. Mr. Conversion ain't been holl'n at his girl lately? What nigga? U feel'n some kind of way about our night together? Dnt front...keep it real ;) - Gabriana ~

_____

Gabriana pushed the *Send* command and then ordered another drink. A few minutes later, Gabriana gazed down at her phone. Not really expecting a reply from Khali, surprisingly, she had one waiting.

_____

~ I'm fall'n bac on u...thts y I aint holla'd. In othr words...im good - King Khali~

_____

Gabriana asked the bartender for a shot of Patron. She downed the drink and then replied.

~ Let me tell u sumth'n u hypocrite. Let me send you a reminder...
Do u NOT remember how loud u were singing my praises tht nght in
my bed!!!!!!!! Wassup wit that, huh?...There was nothing "holy" about
what we did or how you was touching me while we were doing it! Now
let's see...wht do they call tht, "LUST," rght?!!! UR NOT SAVED...UR A
FAKE PROPHET!! Thats wht U r!! But ur good on me?! U lame, I dnt
need u and neither does your so-called God!!! ~

Gabriana didn't know it, but in another place across town, that text
message she sent caused Khali to taste vomit as he coughed. She truly
struck a chord. Less than two minutes later, Gabriana received a reply.

~ I AM NOT A PROPHET!!! I NEVER SAID I WAS ANYTHNG BUT
A MAN!!! - King Khali ~

Now Gabriana was starting to feel empowered. She knew she was
pushing his buttons, so she replied.

~ I DNT BELIEVE U! If u were a MAN u wld stand on ur own 2 feet
instd of bow'n on ur knees. U r not who I thght u were...and on top of
evrythng, u sent all those foul msgs to my man behind my bak and thght I
ain't kno abt all tht! U SNITCH...U SUPER FOUL!!!

Gabriana's feelings were more than hurt. She wanted to cry at the bar. Everything had backfired. Ciona and Milan ordered more drinks and shots. They put twenty dollars into the Internet jukebox. After the drinks were gone, the girls were feeling themselves. Gabriana had to use the restroom, so she slid off to go handle her business. Returning back to the bar, she saw that Milan was flirting with some guy who had just purchased all three of the girls re-ups on their drinks. The night went on.

By 9:00, Gabriana was slurring her words. It did not matter because she had pain to drown away. She began talking recklessly about her disapproval of Khali. "I'm saying though, that nigga ain't who he made me think he was. At least Scholar kept who he was one hundred. Khali's just a walking contradiction, fo'real. Them type of people are the worst." Gabriana looked between both of her friends. "But look, tell me what y'all think about him."

"I like Khali—" Milan tried to reply, but Ciona chimed in.

"I can't say that. It's something about him that just seems sneaky to me. Like I don't knooowww, man. That dude come off standoffish and secretive to me. Watch him closely, Gabriana."

"Well, I don't see that," Milan countered with disgust written on her face. "The dude just quiet. Wow. Y'all act like—"

"Nah, kill that. Watch him." Ciona slurped the remainder of the Absolut Citron from the bottom of the martini glass before continuing. "Fo'real girl, I'm not trying to hate on our boy, I'm just saying. But… so…yeah…I don't fully trust him fo—"

"Ciona, you're drunk. And you don't trust no dudes, " Milan fronted. "Don't listen to her, Gabriana."

"Nah, you just trust niggas too much, Milan. You're gullible, and all

159

that liberal trust gon' get you caught up one day. Mark my words." Ciona rolled her eyes away from Milan, and focused them on her other friend. "Anyway, Gabriana, like I was saying, I don't trust people, but I still like Khali. Don't get it twisted. But you know him better than us. You tell us what's up."

Gabriana vaguely told her girls how hypocritical Khali was. When Ciona and Milan asked for more details, Gabriana decided to change the subject. She did not want them to judge her for her part in his mistake.

The time continued to tick away. It had been a while since she checked her phone. Thinking that maybe she had a reply from Khali, Gabriana glanced at her phone's wide screen. There were ten missed calls. "Yeah, this nigga ain't like that talk." She laughed. Opening each missed call, Gabriana became confused. One of those many calls was from Janette. The other nine that followed were from an unknown number that she did not recognize. "Who could *this* be?"

Covering one ear with a finger, Gabriana returned the call to her mother first. Jannette had been in the hospital for the last two days. She dialed her mother's room directly. There was no answer. Jannette was probably sleep, she thought. Stepping outside for some air and privacy, Gabriana called the unknown number. As the line rang, Gabriana thought maybe the number was a Khali. "He probably didn't want me to know he was blowing me up," she said to amuse herself.

"Hello, is this Gabriana?" the woman asked when she answered Gabriana's call.

"How 'bout you just tell me who you are?"

"If this is Gabriana then, honey, you need to tell me right this minute

160

where you are."

"No, why?" Gabriana was drunk and didn't understand what was going on.

The woman slowly explained to Gabriana what the situation was.

Jannette, Gabriana's dear mother had passed.

Chapter 19

The emergency room's receptionist motioned for Ciona and Milan to come over to the administration window. Dr. Maguire was there, waiting to speak with the ladies. He had told them to go ahead home, and that Gabriana wouldn't be leaving with them tonight. The doctor explained to them that Gabriana suffered from a traumatic anxiety attack at the news of her mother's demise. He asked the girls if there were any immediate family members that they could contact on Gabriana's behalf. Ciona told the doctor *they* were her immediate family.

"Well, I'm suggesting that you get Gabriana a psychological evaluation as soon as possible," he replied, then walked away.

~ ~ ~

Gabriana awakened in the dark room. She tried to move, but she was heavily sedated. Watching the door, she closed her eyes and dozed back off. A few minutes later, Gabriana's eyes shot open. She stared out her doorway. The door was now open. She lay there listening to the nurses maneuver around their stations not too far away. As she watched the hall, she noticed a tall man swiftly walk by. Gabriana squinted her eyes. She heard the man speaking in the hallway near the door, but could not understand what he was saying. Gabriana sat up and listened closer. It was as if the man was talking to himself. She continued to listen. Beginning to feel lightheaded, Gabriana frantically searched for the nurses' buzzer, then began to buzz it with alarm. Less than a minute later, a nurse entered the room and turned on the light.

"Are you okay?" she asked.

Gabriana sat up straight, looking forward. Her eyes were wide.

"Honey, talk to me. Are you okay?"

"There's a man in the hall disturbing me. Who is he?"

"Gabriana, you were dreaming. I have been at that station all night and there hasn't been anyone standing near your room." She pointed toward the hall. "There was no man out in the hallway, I assure you. I would have noticed him at this time of night. Listen, it may just be the meds, honey. Try to get some sleep."

The nurse turned the lights back off, exited the room and closed the door. Gabriana laid back. *At least she could have left the light on.* She then returned to her sleep. Suddenly, the male voice was in the room. When Gabriana opened her eyes, there was no one there.

~ ~ ~

Jannette's funeral was a blur for Gabriana. She was unaware of who sat around her or who attended the funeral, period. The once-scary preacher did not even intimidate her this time. Gabriana was heavily sedated on prescriptions. She didn't know if she was crying or laughing. She didn't speak to anyone nor engage in the reception after the burial.

Three days later, Gabriana finally decided to get out of the bed. It was a stormy day and Gabriana couldn't remember the last time she had eaten, so she felt extremely weak. On the way to the kitchen she grabbed her phone from the charger on the living room table. Gabriana had not spoken with anyone since she and her friends departed the funeral services. She searched the phone for Milan's number. Once she pulled it up, she hit the *Call* button, but quickly found out that her phone service had been disconnected. The phone bill was due last week and Gabriana hadn't thought about any obligations. She tossed the phone on the couch.

Once in the kitchen, Gabriana grabbed an Ensure out of the refrigerator. The first sip caused a deep cramp in the bottom of her stomach. Gabriana tilted her head back and turned the can upside down above her. A small percentage actually found her mouth, the rest landed all over her face and the floor. She threw the can across the kitchen and lifted herself from the chair. "Khali," she softly said. Gabriana walked like a zombie back into the living room and sat in front of the computer. She then wrote an email to Khali.

Dear Khali,

I need help. I love you. Mama's dead. Why do you hate me? Where is Scholar, is he in heaven or hell? I miss my daughter. You should have seen her, she looked just like you. Psyche! Actually she looked just like Scholar. LOL! She's dead now so it doesn't matter. If you care, call me. Oops, I'm sorry, the phone is off. HaHaHa, I cannot stand you! Love Gabriana. No, I'm sorry, I didn't mean that. Please help me, baby! I need you. I need help and I feel extremely sick. Please come back to me. I can't take it. I'm sorry.

Gabriana sent the message then fell sideways out of the chair onto the floor. She slowly looked around then began wildly kicking her legs. She began screaming in a high-pitch tone, then stopped. The tears started to fall as she erupted into a terrified fit. She sobbed hard as she crawled across the floor to the couch. Gabriana wanted to get on the sofa, but she couldn't find the energy to stand. So she laid there 'til she started drifting. She would scream, then moan, moan then scream. As her cries became whimpers, all of a sudden she could hear. The voice in her head said, *Fear not.* Gabriana frowned, then laughed hysterically. The room grew quiet. Suddenly there was another voice speaking to Gabriana. The voice said, *You are all alone, go be with Scholar. He's waiting for you on the other side.* Gabriana looked at her right wrist. She stared at the razor cuts. "You came back," she said to the latter voice before falling asleep on the floor. While sleeping she dreamed.

165

The little girl shot up in her bed. She had to use the restroom urgently. The little girl hopped up and looked into the hallway afraid. Slowly, she got up and exited the safety of her room. She crept toward the bathroom and stood before the door which was slightly ajar. Approaching the crack of the door, she saw a slight glow. Trembling, she entered slowly. Inside all was dark, and there was no glow remaining. She tried to turn on the light, but it was not working. Then she heard the door close. The little girl spun around and saw the lady. Her hair was white like a bright light. It was very thick and long. The child could not see the lady's face. She only made out her silhouette. The hands reached out and the glow began to grow. Terrified, the child fell to the floor, covered her eyes and screamed a deafening siren. Someone was now tugging her hair from behind. The little girl cried harder and refused to remove her hands from her eyes. The tugging stopped. Suddenly, someone was now grabbing the back of her neck and she could feel nails. No longer able to take it, the little girl got up and ran forward. Someone then gently grabbed a hold of her hands. The hands that intertwined with the child's were warm. There were no nails. The hands tugged her forward. The child began to walk with her leader. Then the child stopped. The hands began to tug at hers again. The woman figure spoke. "Gabriana." The accent was unheard of to the young child. Her intrigued mind wanted to look at the lady, but she was too afraid. Then there was a slither behind the little girl. The woman spoke again. "Beloved child, that which you fear is behind you. Look forward." The little girl still refused to open her eyes. Again, she heard the slithering object behind her and jumped. "Look and see what is in store for you. Open your eyes." The trembling child opened her mouth to speak, but the slithering behind her made her feel paralyzed. "Speak," the woman demanded. The child finally said, "Mommy. I want my mommy." The woman told her gently, "Your mother awaits you, but first you must come and see what is for you. Open your eyes." The child replied, *"I can't."* The woman said, *"Yes, you can."* The child tried to squeeze down on the gentle hand, but it was no longer there. The child gasped, then opened her eyes.

Gabriana awoke to someone knocking on her door. Confused, Gabriana touched the mess on her face. "What happened?" she whispered. The knocking grew louder until Gabriana reached the door and opened it. The mail carrier stared at Gabriana with a look of surprise. Regaining his professionalism, he asked Gabriana to sign for the package. She did. Returning to the couch, Gabriana heard the alert on her computer. Looking up at the workstation then back down at the package on her lap, she decided to open the package.

Inside of the envelope was the deed to her mother's house. There were also some other papers. Jannette's lawyer had forwarded the paperwork to Gabriana. The computer's alert sounded again, while she flipped through the stack of hard copies. This time Gabriana checked her messages. There was pending mail from Khali.

~ Gabriana,

I don't know what was going on in your head when you wrote that email you sent me, but listen to me. I'm going to need you to be strong. I know about Jannette's passing because I was there at the funeral. I knew about her passing before you did because I was there when she took her last breath that night. You did not acknowledge me at the funeral or the burial and I understand. I can only image what you are going through, but regardless, you're going to have to find your help. There is a help that you need that I cannot provide. Besides, I am preoccupied. Gabriana, this is what else I want to talk to you about. I have a wife, and I love that woman very much. I have to become a better man in order to be there for her the way God has intended for me to. So, in other words, I have to fall back from you. Don't get offended Gabriana, but you have some demons that you need to slay. I have always felt them surrounding you. See, before I actually met you, I saw you in a dream. In fact, you had been in many of my dreams. In those dreams you would tell me many things that you have never actually told me in "real life." Yeah, I know right? Anyway, in those dreams, I never actually saw your face because the young woman always kept her back to me, but I still knew it was you when I met you. Yeah, real talk, I knew it was you that night at Lights because of one thing. That one thing was a feeling in my gut. That poem I spit that night, I freestyled that. In the first dream, you told me that you were a dreamer. So that night, I freestyled about a dreamer. I figured that if you responded then you were definitely the one from my dreams. I guessed that I was correct when you gave me a call. Although, we never discussed that freestyle, I know those words I spoke had to touch something within you because why else did you call me when you clearly was not feeling me at first? Anyway, look, I'm praying for you nonstop. I apologize for the way I treated you the last time we exchanged texts, but the whole time you were texting me garbage, I was by YOUR mother's side, and where were you? Somewhere trippin!

Look, love can never be lost between us, only found, so forgive me, but I got to get my own self right for my wife. My love for her is more important to me than our little friendship. Please understand. Take care and please, turn to God. He is waiting to guide you. Love Khali ~

Chapter 20

Six weeks later

Gabriana concluded her prayer and rose from her knees. She then
showered and threw on a pair of ripped Rocking Republican jeans, a fit-
ted white tee and short snow boots. Curly hair thrown back into a ponytail, Gabriana grabbed a short red bomber jacket out of the closet and
headed out the door. She was feeling pretty good this morning. Gabriana
wanted to get to the salon early. Tomorrow night, she and the girls were
going out to celebrate Milan's 29th birthday. Gabriana had planned her
day out—salon then mall. She wanted to get her preparations out of the
way, so she could relax.

Over a month ago, Gabriana decided to take Khali's email for what it
was worth. It wasn't that she didn't care about the revelation of his wife;
she was just numb. When Gabriana thought about how Khali never once
took her to his home, or introduced her to his family, it all made sense.
As far as Khali's other confessions in that email, Gabriana really didn't
know what to make of them. However, what she did consider was Khali's
suggestion that she find God. So that's what she decided to try and do.
One prayer at a time, Gabriana slowly began to gain her strength back.
Her appetite returned with a vengeance and she even picked up a little
weight.

DaVon, the beautician, added long tracks to Gabriana's mane as she
requested. Putting his own twist on things, DaVon flat-ironed the tracks
and then added dark-brown highlights. He then pulled and pinned the
middle of the hair up while leaving the sides and the back hanging. Gabriana was looking good and feeling better than ever. She paid DaVon for
his services and left the salon. On her way to the mall, Gabriana began to

think about the dream she had the prior night. It was an uneventful one, but she got to see her mama.

Gabriana was laid out on the couch, watching Jannette read the large Bible. They never spoke. Every few seconds, Jannette would look up at Gabriana and smile, but Gabriana's eyes were fixed on the Bible. There was folded notebook paper cluttering the pages. "Mama, what's on those papers," she asked her mother. Jannette looked over and said, "Come and see."

As Gabriana drove, she thought about Jannette's house and decided to detour her mission. Gabriana had not been back to that house since her mother died.

Gabriana felt a rush as she stepped inside the house. There was little furniture there and a slight stale smell lingered in the air. Jannette's lawyer, and one of her close friends, had arranged for most of the furniture to be removed and given to charity. The house felt abandoned. After glancing around, Gabriana made her way up the stairs and headed into her mother's old bedroom. "Fear not," she whispered to herself. The room was empty, except for a few boxes of paper and clothing scattered around. Gabriana tilted two of the boxes sideways to the floor. She sat Indian style before the boxes and began to review the contents within them. She pulled the papers and books onto the floor and her lap, but did not see what she was searching for. "Where is it?" she asked, staring at the entrance of the door. Gabriana lifted a large picture of herself as a child. The little girl looked so innocent and content as she posed in her off-white dress. The Easter basket was clutched in her hand and she was smiling. Gabriana giggled.

Just as she was beginning to daydream, she thought she heard a noise. Shaken back into reality, she looked up at the doorway. As she stared into the hallway, she heard it again. It was a loud thump. Like something had fallen. Gabriana knocked everything off of her lap and stood. She thought about the bathroom down the hall. That is where the noise seemed to come from. Gabriana's old childhood fear gripped her and she couldn't move. After a moment of silence, Gabriana took a few steps toward the doorway, and then paused. A slight whimper escaped her lips as she stared into the hallway. *What was that? I have to get out of here,* she thought. *On the count of three...1...2...*

Gabriana shot out of the room toward the stairs. She tried not to look toward the cracked bathroom door, but she did anyway. In a split second she spotted it.

The old Bible was on top of an out-of-place china cabinet that one of the movers had left in the hall, near the bathroom. Gabriana froze at the top of the stairs. Her eyes were fixed on the book. "Oh, my God," she said. Gabriana glanced at the bathroom door, then back up at the Bible. Just as she was about to ease toward the china cabinet, she thought that the bathroom door had moved. Fear took over and Gabriana ran down the stairs like an Olympic gold medalist. She ran straight out the door, slamming it behind her. A panic-stricken Gabriana jumped from the porch and ran right into the old woman.

Once Irene got Gabriana to calm down, she told her that she was an old friend of Jannette's. Irene was also a neighbor. She convinced Gabriana to come inside her home.

"When I saw you pull up and enter that house, I said to myself, 'Look at that girly. I had been watching and waiting for you to return for almost two months now."

Seated on the old-fashioned tan sofa, Gabriana watched Irene pace before her. The old woman had very smooth shiny skin. It was almost as if she used Vaseline as a daily moisturizer. Regardless, the old woman carried a beautiful demeanor of wisdom. Irene's hair was dusty black with long consistent strands of gray hair. Gabriana took a deep breath. "I don't understand. Why? What was…I'm sorry…why were you waiting on me, Miss Irene?" Gabriana then laid her face in her hands. She was overwhelmed.

Irene said, "Child, that don't even matter right now. What I want to know is why you came flying out that house like a bat?" She stood over Gabriana and removed her face from her hands.

Gabriana didn't care if the lady thought she was crazy or not. She went on to explain what happened next door. She even explained to her the whole reason she had returned to the house in the first place—for the Bible.

Fortunately, Irene did not judge Gabriana. She simply pulled her up from the sofa and held both of her hands. "Let's go get it then."

Gabriana looked at Irene like she had lost her mind. She was about to reject in words, but instead she just shook her head. "I can't." The look on Gabriana's face expressed pure fear. The old woman stared her right in the face with much compassion. "Fear is not of God," she said sternly, as if she were talking to the devil himself. Irene then released Gabriana's hands and went over to a mantle mounted into the living room wall. There were pictures of relatives scattered about the long shelf. Irene removed a set of keys from behind the picture of a young boy. She then exited the house to go retrieve the Bible herself.

Chapter 21

Gabriana sprayed a light coat of sheen onto her hair then ran her fingers through it. "Still looking good," she said to the mirror while greedily rubbing the palms of her hands together. She smiled as she thought about how Scholar used to perform that same silly vain gesture before the mirror while admiring his reflection. Next, she applied her favorite shimmering nude lip-gloss. She was ready for the night. Gabriana wore a black off-the-shoulder sweater dress with baby leather peep-toe booties. She decided against the leggings and wore her shining legs bare.

Gabriana entered the small hole-in-the-wall lounge and removed her coat immediately. *Freddie Jackson* was crooning "You Are My Lady" through bass-tweaked speakers. Majority of the crowd were older customers, but there was also a nice amount of young patrons, too. Gabriana smirked at the scene. It was what it was, but it had swagger.

"Sexy," Ciona joked.

Gabriana hung her coat on the back of the highchair at the round table where Ciona and Milan were already seated.

"Happy Birthday, Milan, you look hot," she told her friend then hugged her.

"I know, girl, but you always there with me. I'm loving the dress," Milan shouted a little too loud over the music. Gabriana smiled as she looked her friends up and down. "Dang, fo'real, y'all, we killing it in this little spot," she had to admit.

Both Ciona and Milan also wore short dresses. Ciona's was a little tight ocean-blue BCBG, and *Milan* a crème and black Dior draped dress.

The fabric hung off one shoulder while material for the other shoulder was nonexistent. Everything about it was classy. Gabriana could not take her eyes off of Milan. The dress was so fly that there was no need for accessories. Still, Milan wore a single black sequined bracelet on her wrist, and black diamond studs in her earlobes. Gabriana gleamed at the breathtaking ensemble that she had purchased for her friend to shine in on her special day. Milan was stunning and Gabriana was proud to have her back in her corner.

Milan was high-yellow, Creole and thin-faced. Both she and Gabriana were equal in height and pizzazz. Milan carried herself with her head high at all times, but Ciona was the much more humble friend. Her face was round and youthful. She wore deep wavy locks in her mane, courtesy of Milky Way Weaves, and always kept it tight. But Milan didn›t believe in fake hair. She wore her own Spanish-like waves layered over her shoulders with pride. She felt that everyone should follow suit. This night, she wore her usual waves straightened. Only the last inch of her mane was lightly spiraled. She knew she was on point, but Milan had to give it up to Gabriana though. They were running neck and neck. Regardless of Milan›s score, Gabriana always managed to steal the limelight, one way or another. *This girl has always been a problem for me,* Milan kidded to herself. But at the same time, she was dead serious.

Ciona and Milan told the waitress to bring a bottle of Moët and three shots of Patron.

"No!"

Gabriana tried to catch herself, but it was too late. Everyone looked at her with weird expressions on their faces. "I mean…what I mean is…I'm not drinking that hard tonight. I'm driving."

"Well, I'm a professional at drunk driving and I will take you home if need be," Ciona stated.

Disregarding Ciona's comment, Gabriana told the waitress, "Nope, all I want is some Merlot."

The girls got tipsy too fast. They were dancing around the table and having a good time. Then, Gabriana's eyes started blurring a little. *Man, I shouldn't have had that third glass of wine.*

Two dark-skinned dudes made their way to the ladies. The first dude approached them first and introduced himself as Duggy. He looked a little rough, but he still had his swag game up. He was definitely a sexy piece of milk chocolate to a drunk girl. The second dude, who said his name was Maxx, was not really good looking, but he wasn't bad looking either. His bronze face was a little bumpy, head kinda big, but his hair lining was crisp, and he was college-football thick with tattoos everywhere. Both guys had there gear game up and they wasted no time asking the girls what they were drinking. The girls were soon refilling for the fourth time.

Gabriana was drunk and she started to feel nauseated. Her head began to spin. "I'll be back," she said to her two drunk friends who were dancing all over the two guys. Once in the bathroom, Gabriana barely made it to the toilet before hurling. "Oh, my God," she screamed as she flushed the toilet. At the sink freshening up, Gabriana heard her cell phone ringing inside her purse. She retrieved it and answered.

"Hello?" she said, wiping her mouth with a wet paper towel.

"Gabriana, baby? Where are you at, sweetheart?" Irene asked.

"Out with friends, is something wrong?"

"Well," the old woman paused, "I know it's late, but…"

It was only a little after 9:00pm.

Irene continued, "I would like for you to get over here as soon as you can. I want to have another talk with you."

Gabriana thought Irene was tripping and just really wanted some company. However, she obliged. She told her that it would probably be around 10:00 before she could reach her.

"Well, hurry," Irene said before disconnecting the call.

Wow, is she really just gonna rush me like that. Dang, old people, wow." Gabriana wasn't really tripping. She was ready to shake the spot anyway, so she returned and reached for her coat.

"What the—? Girl, where do you think you are going?" Ciona and Milan yelled.

"I'm ready to go," Gabriana replied casually.

"Fine, we can go, but you coming with us back to my house. Maybe we can even find another spot to see about later. It's my birthday, girl," Milan stated loudly. "The night ain't over."

"Milan, you stay too far. How do you know I feel like doing all that driving?" asked Gabriana.

Ciona interrupted their exchange. "No, here's the deal. You're going to leave your car here and ride with me. I will drop you back off at your car on my way home."

The plan did make sense since Ciona lived right around the corner from the lounge. Not wanting to disappoint Milan on her birthday, Gabriana agreed. The crew made their way outside and headed to Ciona's car. Knowing her own automobile was secure because she had paid for parking on a private lot down the street, Gabriana rode off with Ciona and Milan. No worries.

~ ~ ~

Back at Milan's house, Gabriana, Ciona and Milan were sharing their second blunt. The Jay-Z's CD was blasting and the girls were loud, yelling back and forth between one another. Milan's family was wealthy, so they helped to financially keep her home blushed. Her father was an international corporate attorney from Europe, so the girl definitely had plenty of money to dabble in.

Gabriana knew she should not have allowed herself to smoke and drink the way she had that night, but it was Milan's birthday. This was what she told herself. Not long after the girls arrived at Milan's, one of the guys from the lounge began blowing up Milan's cell phone. Milan was feeling loose from all the drinks and the weed, so she invited the guy and his friend over to join the after-party. Ciona was amped up, but Gabriana wasn't really feeling the company. It wasn't that she wanted to be the party-pooper; she was just ready to return to her car. She was also feeling guilty about playing Irene. The only reason Gabriana didn't protest the invites for the guys was because it was early. They all had only been at Milan's a little over an hour. The night was still young.

Gabriana was beginning to feel drowsy, so she kicked off her booties to relax on the loveseat. Just then, the doorbell rang. Milan let the guys into the apartment. Instead of Duggy and Maxx coming alone, they arrived with an extra friend. They simply introduced him as "C." Although the new guy looked much younger than her, Gabriana thought the friend was really cute. He had a beautiful peanut-complexion like Scholar once had. His eyebrows were thick and his eyes were dreamy, almost hypnotic. His thick lips remained closed as he acknowledged the ladies with a simple nod of the head. His eye connected with hers, and rested a second or two too long for Gabriana not to notice. "C" seemed thrown off initially. As if recognition invaded his unprepared brain. That was odd. Still, Gabriana was amazed at the cutie-pie in the room. He was

177

definitely worthy of a little attention. So she decided to sit up and at least appear as if she were engaged with the group. As the guys were getting comfortable, Gabriana did take another mental note. She noticed that the guys all had their hands tucked in their pockets, but she really did not make too much out of it.

"Does anyone want something to drink?" Milan slurred. She held the tall bottle of Grey Goose in the air and laughed. The guys declined. Duggy pulled out a bag of weed and began to break down a couple of blunts. Once the cigars were lit and rotating, Gabriana declined the session. Through the smugly fog, she laid back and watched the guests.

Something started to feel awkward.

Suddenly, something was not right. Glancing between Duggy and Maxx, Gabriana began to notice their faces. They did not appear as they had earlier. Their faces seemed distorted in Gabriana's sight. Nervous, Gabriana asked Milan to follow her into the kitchen. Once the two were alone, instead of honestly expressing her concern, Gabriana simply told Milan that she wasn't feeling well and was ready to return to her car.

"Cool," Milan said with a screw-face. She didn't have time to go back and forth with Gabriana. If she was ready to leave then she better figure it out on her own. *Hop in a cab if you so ready to bounce. Just straight up whack and selfish,* Milan maliciously thought as she walked out the kitchen to return to her guests. Gabriana was left standing alone. Taking a deep breath, Gabriana rejoined the group. She reclaimed her place on the loveseat. Shortly after, Maxx took it upon himself to have a seat next to her. Still feeling uneasy and queasy, her knees began to bounce.

"Aye, you a'ight?" he asked. Gabriana did not answer. She just wanted him to shut up. So she figured if she kept her mouth closed, then just maybe this fool would get it.

"Oh, so I see. So you're one of those stuck-up hoes, huh?" Maxx was getting agitated.

Gabriana was offended, but still said nothing. She only looked across the room. At this point, she caught eye contact with the younger guy, "C." He had been just as quiet as she had been.

"Nigga, this hoe over here playing me like I'm lame or something," Maxx told Duggy.

"Aye, don't disrespect my girl like that," Ciona stated seriously.

"Well, your *girl* shouldn't come off like she coming off."

"How is she coming off? She's not even saying anything, so leave her alone." Ciona argued. She was drunk and getting louder.

Gabriana decided to deaden the argument. "Look, it's all good."

"No, it ain't all good. He needs to chill. We're not little girls. We are grown women," Ciona spat.

Duggy finally spoke. "Yeah, it's good, Maxx. Chill, nigga." He then turned his attention to Milan and asked her if he could use her bathroom. Milan, who suddenly had an attitude, and was surprisingly quiet during the altercation, left the room to escort Duggy. Trying to relax her nerves, Gabriana asked Ciona for the blunt. She took a couple tokes and began to choke. Just as she was beginning to feel the effects, she heard Milan's voice loudly demand, "Stop! What are doing? What is wrong with you?" Her voice got closer. "Look, it's time for y'all to leave 'cause y'all niggas tripping."

Moving quickly back into the living room, Milan displayed a look of panic on her face. That quick, at the snap of a finger, everything changed. Duggy was on Milan's tail with an evil grin on his face. She looked to his friends. "Aye, y'all got to go. Get up and get out of my crib." That's when Duggy pushed Milan forward, causing her to fall to the floor. Stunned, Gabriana dropped the blunt onto the hardwood floor. She and Ciona remained still while watching the event unfold.

Duggy looked over at Maxx. "You know what, fam? Let's do this. Let's get these stuck-up hoes!"

It was then that Gabriana noticed that Maxx was stroking the back of her hair. His response to his friend was only a weird giggle. He then grabbed the back of Gabriana's hair tightly. The scene quickly became psychotic, and unreal for the young ladies as Duggy pulled the .357-magnum gun from his waistline.

It all happened so fast.

Gabriana tried to rise up from the loveseat, but Duggy aimed the gun right at her. As she grabbed her stomach and sat back, Maxx clutched the back of her neck with his hand. *She could feel the nails.* Everything seemed completely surreal to Gabriana. Maxx said something to her, but she could only hear her own heartbeat. Duggy pointed the magnum into Milan's face as Gabriana and Ciona watched on in horror. Gabriana felt as if someone was pouring warm water over her. Duggy then began to tell the girls to remove their jewelry and money. The girls did not put up a fight. They did as they were told. During the process, Duggy and Max threatened to kill everybody, causing Milan to cry out loud. Her light-yellow skin turned bright-red and flushed.

"Shut the f—" Duggy started to scream down on Milan, but instead, he opted for the physical approach to make his point.

POP!

He smacked her roughly across her face, causing her head to jerk

180

back. She could not stop crying.

Before Gabriana could give proper instructions to her friend, Duggy began giving orders out to his guys. "You know what? Straight up, I'm about to rape this crybaby right here. Take them hoes in that backroom right there," he ordered as he held onto Milan's neck.

Gabriana and Ciona were both escorted into the guestroom, located near the kitchen.

Milan's shrieks were loud and treacherous as she begged Duggy not to hurt her. The commotion sent chills through the air. Gabriana could not take any more, so she covered her ears with both hands. A couple minutes later, Maxx became anxious and exited the room. Gabriana removed her hands from her ears, but closed her eyes tightly. She could hear Ciona, who was sitting next to her, whimpering in fear. She wanted to do something, but she was terror-struck herself. She could hear the voices of Duggy and Maxx in the other room, talking fast. Only catching a little of the actual words, she overheard Duggy tell Maxx to go get the other girl. Then she heard Maxx tell Duggy, "We gonna have to kill them, so I hope you know that. Nigga, I'm not going back over this." Milan began screaming out louder and begging for her life. It was gut-wrenching, but the two assailants ignored her pleas.

A few seconds later, Maxx returned to the room and grabbed Ciona by her arms. Gabriana watched helplessly as her friend was dragged out, screaming and crying.

Alone. It was just Gabriana and the "quiet" friend they'd called "C." Gabriana began to chant, "Fear not. Fear not."

She did not see "C" watching her intensely. Gabriana's eyes remained closed tight.

"Open your eyes," he finally said to her. After getting no response he walked over to Gabriana and grabbed both of her hands. "C" pulled her up on her feet. Gabriana began to chant louder. With her eyes still closed, she began to speak to "C." "Please, please don't hurt me. I won't tell, please. Please don't hurt me."

Gabriana was now sobbing harder. The young man moved in close to her face and said, "Open your eyes and listen to me."

Through blurry wide eyes, Gabriana looked into the young face. He pointed to the backdoor. Milan's townhouse apartment was uniquely structured, and had its backdoor located in this room instead of the kitchen. "C" pushed Gabriana toward the door. She was looking shocked and confused, so he opened the door quietly for her. Then he shoved her out the door.

"Run," he whispered. "Go."

Gabriana made her escape. At the speed of light, she ran across the yard and hopped over the fence. She ran and ran. She could hear dogs barking, and she heard the gunshot, but she kept going. Her view of the apartment complex was a colorful blur. Like a flash scene out of *The Matrix*.

Gabriana's feet were bare, and the ground was cold, but she was unfazed. She just ran until she was exiting the alley. Across the street she saw a group of older people standing outside of an old-school juke-joint bar. Gabriana screamed out to those people as she ran toward them. "Help me, help me, help me!" The words exited her mouth, sounding like an ancient Indian chant.

As a dark-skinned older man clutched her body, Gabriana began to feel the cramps. She felt the blood release and pour down her bare legs. The people were getting louder in her ears, but Gabriana did not comprehend. The cramps felt so dreadfully familiar. She screamed as her body released a blob of matter that shook her to the core.

"Not again. No, God, please, not again," she screamed before collapsing to the ground.

Gabriana was unaware at that moment that the gunshot that she had heard was a shot released into the air by the young man, "C," who had helped her escape. He had let off the shot in an attempt to gain the attention of his comrades. When Duggy and Maxx heard the gunshot they removed their attention from the girls. When they entered the backroom, they were surprised to see the back door open and their homeboy standing outside. As the two dudes stepped outside to inquire with the third about what had just happened, Ciona and Milan made their own escape out the front door.

Chapter 22

For three days, Milan stayed at Gabriana's condo. Duggy and Maxx were never apprehended. When the police tried to trace the phone number that the guys had contacted Milan from that night, it came back under a fictional name. Too shaken to return home, Milan camped out at Gabriana's spot ever since.

Gabriana lay in her bed crying quietly. She didn't want to wake Milan, who was lying next to her, asleep. Gabriana thought about Khali and their baby that she had miscarried three days ago. She wept harder when Pastor Hill's sermon on the wages of sin replayed in her mind. Another innocent life destroyed because of *her* mistakes. *My children have paid for my sins. Maybe this is my punishment.* As she reached on her nightstand to grab another Kleenex, she heard Milan speak.

"Stop crying, Gabriana," she said softly.

When Milan awakened, she laid totally still, listening to her friend cry. Her own tears began to drench the sheet underneath her face. Milan made no sound until now.

At the sound of Milan's voice, Gabriana sat up in the bed. Milan also sat up. For a second, the two of them looked at each other in the eyes. Then Gabriana broke down completely. Milan scooted closer and hugged her tightly.

"Oh, my God," Gabriana shouted out in frustration and pain.

"I know, I know," Milan soothed as she cried, too. Both Gabriana and Milan cried until they could not anymore.

"Tell me everything that you have been keeping inside," Milan told her friend.

For those last three days, Milan had done nothing but cried herself. She was devastated about the rape. Gabriana was there for here every second. She listened to every vent Milan released. So now Milan wanted to return the favor.

Gabriana wiped underneath her eyes, then across the bottom of her nose with the wadded tissue. In intimate detail, she went on to explain everything that had happened between herself, Scholar and Khali. The only thing that Gabriana left out were the dreams, and part of the truth. Scholar had taught Gabriana well. She would not be telling anyone everything. Certain other things were simply not to be discussed.

"Gabri, that dude does not hate you. He loves you," Milan said.

While sniffling, Gabriana shook her head no.

"Yes, he does! It's all in his freaking beautiful round eyes," Milan tried to joke. She giggled a little then continued. "When you weren't looking, all that nigga Khali would do was stare at you with this wanting look in his eyes. Both, Ciona and I would always catch him doing so. Once, we confronted him about this, in a joking way of course, but he became serious and admitted it." Milan smiled and pointed her finger at Gabriana. "Gabriana, Khali confessed to us that he loves you very much, but that you did not love him."

Again, Gabriana shook her head in disbelief.

"It doesn't matter anyway. He already has a wife," she replied.

Milan contemplated this and admitted that Gabriana was right. The only thing she could tell Gabriana was to believe that everything was going to get better. "It's gonna be okay," she reassured.

An hour later, both Gabriana and Milan were still awake. Milan lay upside down next to Gabriana, who was picking at her fingernails. Milan had poured herself a glass of white wine, and as she sipped, she began to think.

"Gabriana, can I ask you something?"

"No, but go ahead," Gabriana joked. She pushed her foot toward Milan's glass. Milan swept the foot away. Clearly, Gabriana was feeling a little better.

Milan drained down the remainder of the wine from her glass then looked at Gabriana. "If Scholar had not been killed, do you believe that you two could have worked it out? You know, would the relationship have been able to be maintained?"

Gabriana absolutely had thought about the possibilities herself plenty of times already. She answered honestly. "Because I knew him so well, I would say no." The last word out of Gabriana's mouth cracked.

Milan raised an eyebrow. "Really?" She was a bit shocked by the answer.

"Girl, Scholar had a very huge ego and that ego got bruised. You have to remember that I looked him right in his face and promised him that I would never cheat on him and I broke that vow. To him, I betrayed him and he was devastated. That day when he dropped that ring on the floor that was his way of also dropping me." Gabriana paused to swallow. "Milan, that was his way of breaking up with me," she admitted for the first time. "I mean, sure he could dish it out, but like most typical males of his stature, he could not take it being dished back in. I think my only possible saving grace would have been the pregnancy."

This was Milan's chance. She briefly pondered why her friend did not mention the beating she had taken to be a contributing factor for non-reconciling. But instead of going there, Milan went somewhere else on Gabriana.

"Just going off of everything you told me tonight, did you ever wonder for a second, if Khali was really Skylar's daddy?"

"No," Gabriana answered quickly. She couldn't believe Milan had just asked her that.

The air in the room grew thick and quiet for a moment, then Gabriana spoke calmly.

"Milan, you need to listen more closely. I said I slept with Khali almost a full two months after I returned from being out of town with Scholar. I already had my questions. I know I told you how unprepared me and Khali were when we had sex and to be honest, yes, there was a small ratio of probability, but don't get it twisted. That probability was just too small to count. First of all, I had run out of my birth control while out on the road. During that time was when I got pregnant," Gabriana lied.

"So you're saying that you knew you were already pregnant when you got with Khali?" Milan questioned.

"I mean, my period never returned after I stopped taking the contraception. And it's not like I had the time to see a doctor. After I returned home, it was almost two months later when I first *really* started having some suspicions. Dude, I contemplated the thought before Khali ever touched me," Gabriana stated defensively. After a short moment, she continued in a calmer tone. "I wasn't sure though, and I didn't really want to think about it. Part of me wanted to assume that the awkwardness of my cycle was normal for someone coming off of birth control. I don't know. I really didn't spend too much time dwelling on it when I got with Khali. It was definitely a lot of confusion going on inside of me at the time, but what I do know is that I was with Scholar way more than that one-time event with your boy. Trust, the thought of pregnancy had already crossed my mind prior to our time. So, therefore, Scholar's chance of fatherhood was like two hundred to Khali's one. Second of all—"

Milan tried to hold a straight face as she played along. She knew Gabriana was lying through her teeth. Nothing she was saying added up. If Gabriana was pregnant on the road, plus the months when she was home, she would have been pretty much due by the time she gave birth to her daughter. From what Milan had always understood, she thought that Gabriana had delivered her daughter prematurely. At least, that's what she had heard. Still, Milan went along with everything just to see how far Gabriana would take the fictitious story.

Milan cut Gabriana off and pressed the issue. "You only suspected, but it was never confirmed?"

Gabriana knew where her home girl was going with this, but she refused to let it get to her. She sat straight up and looked Milan in the eyes. "Whatever you're getting at drop it, because I'm certain. When I *saw* her…"

Gabriana stopped mid-sentence as she was briefly taken back. She then concluded, "You know, I had explained to my mama everything that had occurred during that week out in Miami. She told me that Scholar's uncharacteristic behavior could have been a result of what the old women call "male symptoms." When a woman is pregnant, sometimes the child's father experiences some of the same flipside emotions and symptoms that the mother feels."

Milan wandered in space briefly. Finally, she responded, "Yeah, I've heard of that before. That may truly explain some of what Scholar was

189

feeling. I mean, that on top of the stress, plus the tip-off from Khali at the end was a lot."

Milan held her breath, and then released it. She concluded, "You know what else the elders say?"

"What's that?" Gabriana asked dryly.

"That sometimes people can feel death coming for them."

Gabriana didn't say anything in response. Suddenly, her ears felt clogged. She just quietly lay backward and let the tears roll. Within a few short seconds, Gabriana's chest heaved so hard it hurt. Somber reclaimed the atmosphere as if it had never left. Gabriana squeezed the sob through a huge lump that was caught in her throat. Then the words followed. "Oh, my God, Milan, it hurt so bad!"

Milan stared down at her friend's face; she saw the pain, but said nothing.

"I miss him so much. I just want to touch him, Milan. Just one more time I just want God to give him back." Gabriana cried harder as she looked upward, then folded the crease of her forearm across her face to block her eyes from Milan. She drained the words from her heart over and over. "I miss him. I miss him so much. I want him back. Please God."

Milan curled herself down to lay her head on Gabriana's legs. She couldn't look at her friend break down again. She let Gabriana sob it out for a couple of minutes, then she began to softly counter Gabriana's plea to heaven. "Let it go friend. Let him go."

When Gabriana softened her cry and shut down her voice, she could finally hear Milan. "Let him go, he's with the Lord now. You have to move on. Let him go because he's gone, Gabriana."

Milan's words were soothing but real, and for Gabriana, she welcomed them.

Once Gabriana's outburst was settled, there was a peace that stilled the room, and both girls got lost in it. Their latter conversation went on mental rewind in their separate minds. Gabriana hated the way she had to lie to her best friend, but when it came to certain details, she was not willing to go there with anybody. Not Milan, or anyone else, ever. Once Milan was out cold, Gabriana laid there in another world. She closed her eyes and thought of the special things about Scholar, like his favorite song, Stevie Wonder's "Blame It on the Sun."

He told her that he had loved that song since he first overheard it as a teenager. No one knew, but Gabriana, that he listened to it at least once a week. It had been a ritual since he was fifteen. Initially, when he told her about the song, he mentioned that the lyrics were his own confession. He admitted that he had never told anyone that before. She smiled, thinking about when he told her how excited he'd been when he learned that The Fugees had remade the hit. Scholar was Lauryn Hill's biggest fan, period. Nobody was touching her to him, and that was just how he felt. Gabriana wasn't jealous at all by that fact. It only made her study the music that much harder, and love L-Boogie that much more. She knew Scholar had a deeper side to him, yet she never tapped into it. Not fully, like she should have. That was her biggest regret. Their love had seemed so real, so authentic, yet so incomplete. As Gabriana hummed the lyrics of the song to herself, she wondered what type of thoughts went through Scholar's mind as he laid there dying. She wondered what he heard, and what he saw, and even what he felt. Then, she thought about the prayer of forgiveness that she had sent to God on his behalf the night before he was killed. She also thought about what Milan said and wondered if God had acknowledged that sincere request. *"Did God forgive him? Is he really with the Lord now?*" Gabriana asked those tough questions in her mind and waited for answers. There was no audible voice, but the peace in the room did not waver. It remained perfectly still, so Gabriana drifted off into it. She continued to hum the song to herself until finally she felt a comfort wash over her. It was a feeling unlike any she had ever felt before. So with that, she was finally able to sleep like a baby.

~ ~ ~

The following day, Milan finally decided to return to work. Gabriana was left alone. While cleaning up her condo, she thought of Irene and decided to give her a visit.

Gabriana glanced over at Jannette's house as she stepped out of the car. There was a *For Sale* sign now posted in the front yard. "Unbelievable," she said to herself. Don Gionne, her mother's lawyer, had been taking care of all the business for the property. Gabriana really didn't have to do a thing. Jannette had purposely set up things this way. She had known her time would come, and not being sure of how her daughter would be doing mentally, she had made the proper arrangements on her own behalf. The only thing Gabriana was left to deal with was the remaining funds from the insurance check. Don had paid for the funeral with the money himself. Jannette had issued him as the beneficiary. He promised her that he would take care of the funeral cost then turn over whatever was left to her daughter.

Gabriana rang Irene's doorbell at least ten times. There was no answer. "Ughhh," she moaned aloud as she was turning to leave the porch. Looking down at the steps, Gabriana heard Irene say, "So, you finally made it, child?"

Gabriana looked up to see Irene standing in the gangway on the side of the house. "Come, follow me," she said as she disappeared toward the backyard. Gabriana made her way to the back, too.

The yard was huge and gated off by a tall wooden fence. However, Gabriana could still see the back porch to Jannette's house. As Irene was putting her gardening supplies into the small shed, Gabriana could not help but notice the beautiful arrangement of flowers lacing every which way along the bottom of the gate. She was awed. Taking a seat on the wooden steps that lead to Irene's back porch, Gabriana said, "This is absolutely beautiful."

Irene closed the shed up and walked over to the steps. She took a seat next to Gabriana before responding. "It's always been here, honey."

Gabriana looked over at the old woman and replied, "Really?"

"Yep, you gotta start opening your eyes young lady," Irene told her.

"Hmmm, now if I had a dollar for every time I heard that one," Gabriana mumbled to herself.

Irene had very unique hazel eyes. They glistened and stared into Gabriana. "Tell me something, Gabriana, what do you want for yourself?"

Gabriana was caught off guard because no one had ever asked her that before. "Honestly, I never really wanted too much. All I wanted to do was marry Keon and have his children," she confessed with a faint giggle. "I wanted a family because for so long it had just been me and my mama. I mean, I'm sure you've heard our story. My mama was a foster kid. She never knew any of her family. She never had, or even met a mom or dad. No grandparents, aunts, uncles, cousins—none of that. Nobody existed but me and her. So yeah, I wanted a real family."

Gabriana stared off. She was being completely honest with Irene. For some reason, she felt like it was okay to do so.

"Well, where is this Keon and why aren't you his wife?" Irene asked.

"He was killed." Gabriana sighed.

She went on to give Irene a brief description of her time with Scholar and the events that had taken him away. "I mean, Irene, we almost made it there. I was pregnant, but we didn't know. But still, the whole time he was planning on proposing. I still have the ring. It is soooo beautiful. I just get so mad just thinking about it all. Ughhh."

Irene looked out into her yard, and then said to Gabriana, "Hush now, child, it wasn't a part of the Lord's plans, because if it was it would have carried through. Wouldn't have been a thang the devil could have done to stop it. If y'all would have had y'all faith up in the Lord, He could'a guided y'all. But y'all went and did things y'all own way. Therefore, the devil had his way. At least to a certain extent he did." She glanced over at Gabriana who was looking down at her feet. "Hold your head up. Ain't no sense in having no pity party. You just gon' have to accept it. That was your will, *not* His. Good thing about it all is that in the good Bible, our Lord God teaches us that 'All things work together for good.' That's according to His will if you love Him. Gabriana, do you love the Lord?"

"Irene, I'm gonna be absolutely honest with you here. I don't even know what the word *love* means anymore."

Irene smiled, then folded both hands on top of her lap. Gabriana just watched her.

Irene quoted loudly, "Corinthians, Chapter thirteen, it tells you right there." Gabriana squinted her eyes as she listened to the old woman slowly continue her speech.

"Love is patient and love is kind; love does not envy; love does not parade itself, is not puffed up; does not behave rudely, does not seek its own, is not provoked, thinks no evil; does not rejoice in iniquity, but rejoices in the truth; bears all things, believes all things, hopes all things, endures all things. Love never fails."

Gabriana never took her eyes off of Irene. "Irene, that was beautiful, and real. How did you come up with that?"

Irene laughed and patted her legs. That was funny to her. "Child, that ain't me. I just told you, that's Corinthians. Go read it for yourself."

Gabriana had a blank look of confusion on her face.

Irene looked at her and laughed again. She then said to Gabriana, "From the Holy Bible, child. That's the words of the good ol' faithful Bible."

The verse made Gabriana think. She thought of the relationship she had shared with Scholar. Then, she thought of the friendship she had shared with Khali. "So that's what God says love is, huh?"

"That's exactly correct. And if anyone tries to convince you otherwise, don't believe 'em. For they know not what they do or the truth."

Gabriana wanted to tell Irene about Khali, but wasn't sure. So instead, she asked her, "What does it mean when the Bible tells us to be *still*?"

Gabriana asked this question because she remembered her mother always telling her this. Also, Khali had said this to her on more than one occasion.

"It means to be at peace. To let go and let God. It means to stand in place and wait for instructions and guidance."

Irene stood to her feet, and then turned toward her backdoor. "Get up and follow me inside, girl."

Chapter 23

Irene stood in the middle of the living room as Gabriana took a seat on the couch. She had noticed the change in the old woman's demeanor and was becoming a little nervous.

"You know me and your mother went way back?" Before Gabriana could respond, Irene continued. "You were always busy with your friends, so on lonely days your mother would come sit with me over here and vice versa."

Irene stared at Gabriana with such intensity that it sent cold chills through her whole body.

Irene said, "Stand up, child."

Without hesitation, Gabriana stood.

"Look around."

Gabriana stiffened and looked at Irene with bewilderment.

"I said, look around. Look around and tell me what in here looks familiar to you," Irene demanded.

Gabriana looked around the living room briefly, then turned her attention back to the old woman.

"Look carefully," Irene instructed in a slow tone.

"I don't…" Gabriana began slowly walking in circles around the large room. She looked about the furniture, then the shelves. Nothing. So next, Gabriana looked around at the figurines scattered about on the small tables, and then she looked up at the mantle.

Gabriana stared a little longer this time. Her eyes slowly traced the pictures above the mantle, and then the many frames on top of it. She noticed the picture of the young boy, but shook the thought and turned about-face toward Irene.

There was about a good two feet between Gabriana and Irene. "I don't see anything. I don't understand what is going on," she said to Irene.

"One more time, look around one more time."

This time, Gabriana did not budge from her position. She stood completely stiff and looked into Irene's face, as Irene returned the gaze.

Then suddenly, Gabriana spoke in a whisper, "Oh, my God..." First, she covered her mouth, then placed her hands over her ears as she continued to look into Irene's face.

"What do you remember?" Irene asked Gabriana.

"I...oh, my God," Gabriana said as she moved forward to close the gap between herself and Irene.

"I remember you. I remember your voice."

"Where do you remember my voice from?" Irene asked Gabriana.

Gabriana tried to blink back tears that managed to still appear. Then she closed her eyes and began to speak in an almost hypnotic state.

"I was so young. Only like three years old when I slipped under the water in the bathtub, and standing up in the tub when mama told me over and over not to do that. I remember closing my eyes and seeing nothing but blackness. Then I remember the lady standing over the water. She was tall, yet her face seemed so close to where I laid. She didn't speak a word, didn't even open her mouth, but I could still hear her. I…I don't remember what she said, but I can remember the lady putting her hands into the water and then I could breathe again. Then I heard my mother screaming. My eyes were still closed when I heard the third voice. That voice was praying. Suddenly, I felt the cold breeze of the air, like we were outside. Then nothing."

Gabriana opened her eyes from the memory and the old woman wasn't there. Irene was standing across the living room, staring quietly out of the window. When she spoke, she hesitated then told Gabriana, "Gabriana, none of what you just described ever happened to you."

Gabriana blinked a few times. "What? But—"

Irene interrupted her abruptly. "That was my *own* grandbaby that drowned in that tub that morning, not you." Irene began to slowly pace before Gabriana. "I told Jannette. I warned her," she mumbled on to herself. After a brief delay of thought, she looked up into Gabriana's startled gaze before speaking again. This time her attention matched the salty eyes that watched her through confusion. "Ya mama used to go see that old hag across the street." She swatted her hand angrily. "I told that gal, stay away from that witch. She would just laugh me off and defend that woman. She would tell me, *She's a psychic; she's not a witch, Irene.* She was just as hardheaded and stubborn as I complained you were."

"Who? What are you talking about?" Gabriana questioned, tremors lacing her tone.

"Ya mama and Sister Roha. That's who I'm talking about. Listen to me when I'm talking to you. The woman was a witch! Point blank. That's what them so-called psychics are—witches. I warned her to stay away from that lady. But ya mama became intrigued after that woman told her some information on that crazy daddy of yours, and she just kept

199

running back over there after that. I used to always fuss at her about it 'cause I knew that no good could come of it. My own mama and daddy taught us kids early about them psychics. They either a part of an occult or they directly summon and consult demonic spirits from Hell on their own. Whatever the case be, it's evil witchcraft that they practice."

Gabriana could feel her heart skipping beats. She wanted to interrupt Irene's ramblings, but she was frozen stiff with fear. What exactly was the lady implicating? Just as she gathered the energy to put her tongue into real-time motion, Irene cut her off before any words could be motivated into existence. "Hold on now, don't say nothing," Irene spat. "Just listen on a little bit."

Gabriana impatiently held her peace.

"I warned your mother that messing around with the likes of them types of evil was beyond bad. That mess opens up doors and pathways for spirits to travel through straight from the pits of *Hell*."

It was becoming overwhelming. Gabriana caught and lost her breath all together. She instantly remembered how her mother used to consistently check her horoscope. Every chance she got. On top of that, Jannette had a bad habit of asking everyone that she met for their birthday signs. She even had all kinds of books on astronomy spread around the house. This was the norm, up until Jannette got saved. Then Gabriana remembered her mother throwing them all in a bag. When she quizzed her mother about it, Jannette looked her dead in the eyes and told her, "I'm throwing all this crap away in a trashcan far off somewhere on the other side of town." At the time, Gabriana peeped the stress, and thought Jannette was just being her dramatic self, but still she couldn't help but record the look her mother wore as she spoke those words to her. Her face said urgency, and regret. And now listening to Irene, Gabriana recalled all of this and the pieces began to fit. "I said over and over, time and time again to Jannette, that mess you fooling around with brings on generational curses and all kinds of unnatural stuff. Rid yourself of that lady and quit letting her run those tarot cards and all those palm readings on you, girl. Ain't no good gon' come of it. If you want to know something about anything, you turn to God and patiently wait on *Him* to reveal things to you."

Irene paused. She noticed the shaking hands of Gabriana, and although she didn't regret the knowledge she was sharing, she did not want to cause the young woman fear. She closed her eyelids and asked the Lord for wisdom on how to proceed. Excepting her peace by faith, Irene felt led to continue, but this time more to the point. "Look, I'm not trying to scare you, child. And I don't want to invoke any sideways thoughts about your dear mama. Jannette was later saved and forgiven for all her sins. We can't forget that or dismiss it. But, I can't help…" Irene shook her head defiantly as if she were debating something inside her head. "I can't help but wonder, 'cause of what you just said, and 'cause of everything from your youth, girl. Oh, Lord, forgive me for saying this, but Gabriana I believe because of her dabbling around with that old magic lady, it's just clear that some ol' type of spiritual warfare broke out on her very own child. She didn't know what she was doing or what it would cause. But I seen it all from when it all first started happening."

Gabriana felt nauseated.

"So what are you saying…that I'm cursed?" Gabriana unintentionally began to shout. "You're saying I'm cursed because of something my mama did?" Gabriana's tear-streaked face grew numb by the second. Her tears felt hot and the terror was so deep that she thought she would faint. "Oh, my God, what's happening to me? What's wrong with me?" Her eyes begged the old woman for help, and for hope. Irene did the only thing she could do. She hugged Gabriana. Her arms were so fragile but comforting. The strength in them were not her own. "It's okay, baby. It's

201

okay. There isn't anything for you to fear, you hear me? God is a deliverer. He can break any chains and any yokes. Any curses and all evil. Everything has to obey the name of Jesus."

Gabriana had no clue what Irene was speaking of, but still she found comfort in everything she was telling her. It all sounded hopeful as Irene began to pray silently over her. So she cried a moment, and allowed Irene to nurse her. Moments after the prayer closed so did the torment of fear. Just as quick as they had flooded, Gabriana's tears began to subside. When Irene felt it was safe to go on and relay more information, she released Gabriana from her hold and studied her face. Surprisingly, Gabriana did the same. Irene could see renewed strength on the young lady. Seconds later, Irene said, "My daughter, Carmen, lived next door with your mother at one point. They were best friends since kindergarten. You're mother was pregnant with you at the time. That voice you heard praying was me."

Irene then remembered how she used to always pray over Jannette's unborn child. She then continued.

"You know my grandbaby never recovered that night. After we rushed that child to the hospital the doctors pronounced her dead on arrival. Ya know, for about five years after your birth, I would hang over with the ladies at that house, helping them with the children. See, aside from the baby that passed, Carmen also had other children. Two little boys. The youngest of them was actually the twin of my deceased granddaughter. Well, anyway," Irene continued, "when you were around five years of age, I remember you started having really unique dreams and you would then tell us things about them. When you mentioned to my daughter the same scene that you just described to me, she couldn't take it. Carmen took those little boys and left. I remember she thought whatever mess plagued your mind also started to affect her son. She got on up out of there and left the city altogether." As Irene talked, Gabriana tried to mentally recollect the children. There were fragments of living with other kids, but for the most part, their faces were blotted from her memory. "Carmen stayed away and never returned until your mother informed her of her illness. You know, Gabriana, you were probably the last to know about Jannette's condition. You weren't home much, even after you found out about it, so it was Carmen who comforted her on those lonely nights."

Once again, the tears began to flow from Gabriana's eyes. Throughout all the thoughts that were attacking her mind, Gabriana asked one question. "Where is this Carmen?"

Irene's eyes widened dramatically. "Oh, well, it's funny you ask. That night you were supposed to show up here, but never made it, well that was the night that she was here waiting. After I told her that I had you here in my home, that's when Carmen wanted to meet you immediately. She wanted to reunite with you."

Gabriana wiped her wet face harshly with her forearm.

"Irene, get your things and take me to this woman. She's your daughter; I know you know where she lives, or wherever she is staying."

~ ~ ~

During the drive, Gabriana listened attentively as Irene responded to the new information that Gabriana had decided to enlighten her with. As soon as the car pulled from the curbside, Gabriana went in. She confessed to Irene about the dreams. Not all of them, but she let it be known that she was a dreamer. Now, as she considered the wisdom of the silver-stranded woman seated next to her, the pained inner-child of Gabriana felt a sense of relief. She was more than grateful that she'd decided to reopen her mouth to someone about what sometimes happens at night. For so long, she'd harbored the visions to herself. There was always lack of support and understanding all around Gabriana up until this moment. Now, instead of condemnation, she felt free as Irene allowed her to release the things that were bundled up inside her soul. Gabriana did more than appreciate the ear. With a renewed mind, she tucked away everything Irene was explaining to her into her heart.

Irene comforted her. "I don't doubt whatsoever that many of your dreams may possibly be from the good Lord. He spoke to many people in the Bible through dreams, but also, Gabriana, some of your dreams, I believe, are a direct result of fear. And I don' told you, anything of fear is not of God. You know God by His peace, baby. God is pleased by faith and Satan by fear. Learn the distinction." As if somehow she could read Gabriana's thoughts, Irene added, "Don't be confused, child. God *will* sometimes allow fear to enter your life if that's what it takes to get your attention. But He doesn't like it. Sure He would rather draw you in with love and kindness, that's His Will, no doubt. But sometimes, people just don't understand any other way, but the hard way." The latter of Irene's words dragged, displaying the significance of them.

Gabriana squeezed her inquiry in. "And what's that?" Irene was a talker and would go word for word. Still, to Gabriana's amazement, despite Irene's age, she was swift as an eagle, and sharp like a knife. There was no senility in her whatsoever, only golden wisdom to be relished.

"Listen, girl, and don't ever forget this. Satan is a very real adversary who goes above and beyond to destroy. Don't you know that he doesn't work alone, but he has a kingdom with him? He has appointed all kinds of demonic spirits to roam this very earth we live on. Their job is to accompany him in tormenting and deceiving the minds of the people here. They take possession of people left and right. And the sad thing about it is, most of the people are not even aware that they are being controlled by such spirits."

"Why? And what kind of spirits are you talking about?" Gabriana shot out. She wanted to know more. She frowned heavily because she had never heard of this.

"Because he hates you. That's why. And don't act so dumb, girl. Look around you. Demonic forces bind most of this planet—and the youth. Look at their lust, and way of life. Look at their need for power and money. I mean, heck, look at the way they dress. Boys and men wearing these womanly, feminine clothes. And wearing these silly tight pants. Don't think I don't see that nonsense. It's everywhere. Females running around acting all desperate and immoral. Showing off what's only meant for their husbands to see to every eye with vision by wearing trashy, disgusting attire, and in the sight of a Holy God. That's the worst part. That's not normal. Look at the piercings and tattoos they're wearing. Start asking folks if they know what they mean. Some of that so-called artwork are portholes for these demons that I'm telling you of to travel through. People put stuff all over their bodies not knowing what it is they do. Also, pay attention to the music you're listening to. It's going straight from the ear to the brain. These rappers and singers are giving way to evil spells 'cause they putting out all kinds of works of the devil. If it ain't of God, it's of the devil. And you know what else? I'm not even gonna mention the drugs."

Gabriana found her opportunity to rebut. Her mouth dropped. "Now hold on, Irene. Every generation took part in drugs. It's not just a modern thing."

"That's true. I don't deny that. But it's very wicked, and whew nowadays they just use everything. Something just feels different, child. Like mankind's just under some kind of spell." Irene spoke lowly, but her disgust was well-evident. "I can't quite put my finger on it, but something is deathly wrong out here. The possession of souls is greater now than I ever recalled before. If you really can't see that we are running

205

out of time, then you are truly blinded. But it's more than just the people you know, look at the weather. There have always been bad storms, and earthquakes and such, but never back-to-back like you seeing on the news nowadays. Something is off balance; I'm trying to tell you what God's trying to tell us."

Gabriana took it all in. Her own mother tried to tell her spiritual things before, but never like this. It was something about the way Irene was breaking it down that caught Gabriana's attention fully. Some of what she was learning was very disturbing, she had to admit, but Irene topped it all off with the sweetest icing. "Gabriana, you don't ever have to fear any of this as long as you know your Help."

"But who is my help, God?"

"That's right, baby. But see, this God has a Son, with a name. And it's very, *very* important that you young people learn it. His name is Jesus. Anytime you feel you're in trouble, or grave danger, remember to always call on that name. Say out loud with your mouth, "I plead the Blood of Jesus."

"The Christ," Gabriana whispered aloud. She didn't know much about Him, but she'd definitely heard of Him.

"Yes. He is the Christ and He's more than a holiday. He is the Savior that I was telling you about who can deliver you from those terrifying dreams of yours and also, from the Hell below. 'Cause when we die, we either go up…" Irene pointed her scrawny finger toward the roof of the car. "…or we go down," she pointed down toward the black mats of Gabriana's car interior.

Gabriana understood well where Irene was referencing. In a split second, Gabriana thought about him, then she spoke Scholar's name out loud. She often wondered his final fate.

206

"You young people, your generation seems to have forgotten that, Gabriana. Or maybe they just don't know or get it, but Hell is very real. And I'm not trying to scare you, but the truth is the truth. Look around at the way you see your friends, and others around your age range living. You tell me if you think it's right. Tell me if you think there is no consequence for the defilement you witness going on out here. Satan is busy and he's not playing around. He got y'all all caught up in the love of money, and the power of this world, *his* world, but it's all an illusion, girl. Don't be fooled. What a lot of y'all fail to realize is that when the life y'all love so much is over one young person after the other busts Hell wide open. Guess what Satan is doing while this is happening? He's laughing…he's laughing that evil laugh of his, 'cuz he knows that once the lights go off, and you go down there, you ain't never coming out. That's forever, eternal torment, girl. Now close your pretty eyes and picture that heat."

Gabriana's tongue was glued down. She knew that she too fell into a mass majority of the categories Irene spoke of. With one hand on the steering wheel, the only thing she could do was squeeze tightly around the thin hand that had reached over and squeezed her free hand. She had no defense or argument for Irene's wise observations. Gabriana knew it would be ignorant of her to continue to ignore the signs, and everything the woman was feeding her. But what could she do about any of it?

Again, as if reading Gabriana's mind, Irene came out with words of encouragement. "Gabriana, if you would just give the Lord some consideration and submission, I believe He can use you, and probably those dreams of yours for His use. Just think about this discussion and pray on it later. Okay?"

Gabriana swallowed hard, then with a deep blink of the eyes, she promised, "Okay, I will." She wanted to close the conversation there, but somehow she let loose another utterance. "One day," to that "okay" she had just offered. Irene caught on.

"One day? Now if I had a quarter for every time somebody closed with that one I'd be rich. Tomorrow is not promised to any man. Not one. People have got to get this through their heads. The kingdom of God is at hand and Jesus is coming back much sooner than everyone thinks.

Readjusting herself around the passenger seat as if she were the one uncomfortable instead of Gabriana, Irene concluded, "It's your time, Gabriana. I can feel it. It's time."

Within twenty-five minutes, the BMW pulled in front of the small brick house. The street was residential. It was now midday, and there were a few people going about their business, but for the most part, the Maplewood neighborhood was pretty calm. Once out of the car, Gabriana's heart began to beat like an African drum before war. She walked with Irene up to the door with her eyes never once leaving the black Land Cruiser sitting in the driveway behind the Red Dodge Stratus.

Irene knocked on the door with a force that surprised Gabriana. After a few moments, a petite short woman opened the door. Her pressed hair was pulled into a plain ponytail. Her eyes were gorgeous circles, and her cheekbones sat high on the thin face. By her facial bone structures, it wasn't hard to tell that this woman had some type of rich heritage in her blood. Her skin was a glowing red. The lady only briefly acknowledged the old woman before turning her attention fully to Gabriana.

Before Gabriana knew what happened, Carmen was hugging her tightly. The hold of her wrapped arms squeezed for an extended amount of time.

"Come in," she said, finally releasing Gabriana. Irene followed Carmen inside the home, but Gabriana hesitated. After a couple seconds of delay, she stepped over the threshold and lost her breath.

Khali was on the couch, watching ESPN on a huge flat-screen television. He was wearing a black Seven zip-up hoodie. The hood was thrown over his head, but there was enough of his reddish-brown face exposed to identify him. Initially, he seemed unfazed by the company until he glanced up with round eyes. That's when he pulled the hood off and swallowed so hard that he almost lost air. Something popped in his chest.

Gabriana could not tell if the expression on his eyebrows was one of surprise or anger. She unintentionally dropped her head when Khali sprang to his feet. Gabriana didn't know if he had moved or she had, but someone had because she was now hugging him. They were hugging each other. Disbelief consumed both of them. Gabriana thought of the baby and hugged Khali tighter. Khali didn't know what all had been going on, but he felt a lot of energy.

Irene and Carmen kept quiet. They just watched the scene before them. The only words spoken were that of Gabriana.

"Where is it," she quietly asked after looking down.

Khali did not answer.

"Where is it?" Gabriana repeated. "Where is it, Khali?" Her eyes were now as wide as Khali's.

Again, Gabriana looked down at Khali's bare left hand. She said, "You said you were married. If you are married then were is your ring? Why have I never seen it, Khali?" New hurt formed in her voice. Fury, love, abandonment, pain and desire; all those emotions were in her tone. Caught up, Gabriana did not care about the thoughts of those watching. She needed answers, right away.

Khali looked into Gabriana's eyes. "I said I had a wife, yes."

Gabriana pulled out of his embrace and frowned. She squeezed the bones in his hand. Gabriana wanted him to feel the crushing that was happening to her own heart at the thought of him being under such a sacred commitment during their entire friendship. His hand ached instantly. Khali looked to the puzzled faces of his mother and grandmother, then said, "Excuse us for a minute." He took Gabriana's hand and led her to his bedroom.

Chapter 24

"So this is where you live? You live here with your mother?" Gabriana asked, her attitude apparent.

"No, she's been staying here with *me* since she returned from Philadelphia," Khali replied.

"So Carmen is your mother? And on top of that, you knew my mama the whole time, and neither one of y'all told me? Why?" Gabriana questioned, but Khali held his tongue. "Oh, so you don't have nothing to say about anything, right? Khali, why would you not tell me about your family? That whole time we were friends, you never told me anything."

This time Khali opened his mouth. "Look, Gabriana, you never asked. It's that simple."

Gabriana squinted with displeasure. Her inhaling and exhaling sounded before her reply. "So you have a brother, huh? And you had a twin that died when we were little?"

Khali nodded. "Yeah, I did," he uttered. "I see my grandmother told you about her."

"No. I told her."

Khali caught on instantly, but the statement lingered alone.

"Khali, what is going on here?" Gabriana softly asked then glanced down at his hand.

Khali looked down at his hand, then began to rub his head. He offered the truth saying, "Gabriana, listen. When I told you that I had a wife, I was speaking with my faith. I was trying to speak the non-existing into existence." He stopped to search her eyes.

"Man, what the fu—"

Gabriana was interrupted when Khali moved directly in front of her face. He then gently dropped a peck on her lips.

"Let me finish, okay? I want to finish." Gabriana held her tongue as she followed Khali's mouth. The kiss was unwarranted and simple, but tasteful and missed. It wasn't much, but coming from someone she adored, it was everything wrapped up in a split second. Still there was confusion.

"I knew it was you when I saw you," Khali continued on. "See, just like *you*, I dream, too. And like I told you, I had dreamed of you. I had a feeling it was you the minute I peeped you. So I recited that poem to see if it would catch your attention. And like I told you, it did. What I didn't tell you was that in the dream, where I dreamed of you, you were always the daughter of my mother's friend. I don't know how I knew that, but in the dream, it was a given. So, after—"

"Khali, stop it." Gabriana shook her head. "That's game. You knew who I was the whole time. Irene told me that we lived together when we were kids. So you remembered me from there. I was a little younger than you, so I didn't remember myself, but you were like eight when you moved away. You already knew who I was, so don't run that game. That's the big secret that you and my mother were hiding all along."

"After I actually met you at Lights, the next day I asked my mother about Jannette's daughter. She confirmed your identity and that you were indeed a dreamer. That was the confirmation I needed. There was no doubt anymore," Khali concluded in a spacey state. He was dazed and speaking from his heart. What Gabriana had to say was relevant, but it wasn't the truth, therefore, it wasn't worthy of rebutting. "I knew you from my dreams, and only my dreams," is all he offered. The truth needs no additives for convincing someone.

Overwhelmed, Gabriana stepped backward and sat on the bed. Whether he remembered her as she accused him, or not, in her spirit she really did believe him. Khali had met her on greater terms "in his dreams," just like he claimed.

He went on to explain the reason why he had made the decision to fall back on her. "This is crazy," Gabriana mumbled to herself while he talked.

"Gabriana, I had to be sure, because I wasn't. How could I love someone who loved another man? That wasn't fair, and I didn't know, so I prayed about it. I mean, all the signs were presented but still, I was losing my faith. So then, I mean, but then…"

Khali paused and tilted his head slightly.

His expression became extra serious; he looked into Gabriana's face, hoping she wouldn't snap when he continued. "But then Scholar was killed," he said hoarsely.

The whites of Khali's eyes began to change to pink.

Surprisingly, Gabriana's displayed no reaction. Khali watched her closely, but there was nothing, so he continued.

"So you know, after so many signs and all the coincidences, which I didn't believe in, I still lacked faith because of all the unbelievable mistakes I had made…" His voice trailed off into a whisper before picking back up in volume. "There were just some things on my conscious, and on my heart, that I just could not get past. So I went ahead and made the commitment to God. I needed to redeem myself to move forward," Khali said lowly. "I told God that if He would forgive me, and help me." Khali paused to think about what he was revealing. He then jumped pages.

"I knew something real was going on around me and it was scaring me. I had to make a real commitment in order to really get my redemption. That's why I was crying that day at church. I knew the things that I had done, and I knew what I had to do, I knew." Khali swallowed and rubbed his head with both hands. Gabriana's face was stone. "I didn't want to do it, but it wasn't my will. I was tired of being condemned about everything, so I had to prove myself to God. I had to prove my love to Him and to you."

There, the cat was out the bag. At least, the tail of it was.

Gabriana squinted her eyes as she stared on with Khali.

He then said, "Gabriana."

Khali turned his attention across the room and held his pause. Gabriana stood and walked over to him. She reached up, and pulled his face back toward hers. "Don't look away. Tell me," she demanded.

"*You* are the wife that I told you about, Gabriana."

"What?"

"It's you! It's always been you, straight up. I just had to release you in order to see if you would really be guided back and what more can I say? You walked right through my front door!"

Gabriana was lost for words.

~ ~ ~

Later that night, Gabriana lay in Khali's arms. He reached forward for her hands and held them tight. He leaned close to Gabriana's left ear. Khali then whispered to her, "Are you ready, Mommie?"

Gabriana squeezed Khali's hands tighter. "Yes."

Khali led the prayer as Gabriana bit down on her bottom lip. "Father in Heaven, we first thank You for who You are. We thank You for life and for this moment. With that being said, Father, we ask You for forgiveness, for we have sinned in your sight, and against Your name and Your Will. Please forgive us of every trespass and every mistake. Tonight, I bring before You, Gabriana, who, as You already know, is the love of my life. Together we agree that there is a destiny in our partnership, so we ask for Your blessing to become one. We ask for Your guidance and direction. Together, we want to serve You, but Gabriana does not know You. But by her faith, and with my faith, she is saying that still, she wants to trust You and live according to Your design, and so do I. Please accept her, accept us into Your holy kingdom. Teach us how to pray and how to love one another and You. Right here, we ask all of this in the name of Jesus Christ, our Savior. Amen."

Once they ended their prayer, Gabriana continued talking to God for herself. She said to Him, "Thank you."

Gabriana then turned and hugged Khali. She could not believe this man. So simple, yet so classic and special.

So especially for her.

It was now or never. Gabriana placed her face to Khali's and kissed him with all her heart, soul and might. "I love you, and I can't wait to be your wife, baby."

That was the very first time that Gabriana had spoken such words to Khali, and he locked them in his heart. Forever.

Epilogue

Gabriana drove the BMW down Highway 70, doing seventy miles per hour. It was almost 2:00pm on a sunny, Saturday afternoon. The weather was perfect, like a movie. She lowered the top down and let the air blow through her straightened hair. The wind was calming. It dried her eyes as the tears flowed. As she rode, Gabriana thought of Scholar. She missed him a lot. She even missed his family. At one point in her life, Gabriana would have bet the farm that she would be spending the rest of her life with him. But things didn't turn out that way. Although she had tried to close that chapter of her life, she still thought about him from time to time. She thought about the should'ves, could'ves and would'ves. Gabriana released a long sigh.

Exiting the ramp, Gabriana thought of her mother. What would Jannette have thought about the way her daughter had moved forward? Gabriana even thought about the father that she had only met once. She remembered him being very handsome but quiet the day that they had met. Gabriana was only ten years of age at the time, but she never forgot him. It was something about him. As an excited little child, happy to finally meet her father, she was too young to understand that he wasn't right. Now as she thought about him, she realized why he left them behind. Gabriana's father was a rolling stone. After that first introduction, her mother would not allow her to see him or speak his name again.

Gabriana then thought about Khali. The last three months had been like a dream; and they were the dreamers. But it was real. Khali was more than a man to her. He was a beautiful purpose, an existence that deserved the best out of life. She had come to admire him more and more. Khali had taught Gabriana many things during their friendship, but since he had become her fiancé, things soared to a new height. That day that they were reunited was like a fairytale. Except it was not, it was her life. God had remembered her when he considered Khali. Both Gabriana and Khali did not take this for granted, so Gabriana allowed Khali to lead her with his faith. They were engaged right there in Khali's room. He had gone to a dresser drawer and removed a box. Inside was a small but intimate ring. The ring fit Gabriana's finger perfectly when she accepted his proposal. Khali even got down on one knee. With tears in her eyes, Gabriana accepted. That night she told Khali to help her pray to God. She did not want to make her decision before a crowded church of strangers, kneeling on her knees before the altar. Gabriana wanted to make that crucial decision before God with her man at her side supporting her, just the three of them.

So Khali held her hands and became a witness.

As Gabriana moved the contents from the trunk of the BMW, she continued to think of Khali. "Such a good man, I'm so undeserving of him, Lord," she whispered. Gabriana knew without any doubt that Khali was destined for her as she was for him. Although, life had presented her many twists and turns, they were all valuable lessons in the end. Now, as she thought of Khali and their courtship, she compared him to the Corinthians verse that Irene had shared with her. "You've been so patient and kind to me, baby," Gabriana said aloud. She was truly proud of his growth. With the love and affection that he had been showing her, she caught herself feeling as if her love for this man had grown beyond that which she had once felt for Scholar. It was a deep gratitude that had lured her to that point. Thanks to Khali, Gabriana went from having no family to inheriting, not just a wonderful man, but a mother, a brother, two grandmothers, and a grandfather. On top of all that, she also inherited a host of aunts, uncles and cousins who all seemed excited to meet her. Yes, God had remembered her indeed.

Closing the trunk, Gabriana smiled faintly. The traces from the tears streaked her face. "Wow," she said to herself as the thoughts flowed like a slideshow in her mind. Khali's family had made all the wedding arrangements for the couple's official union. Now three months later, everything was ready to go.

Today was the wedding day of Gabriana Hilson and Khali Simone.

Gabriana laughed to herself again as she placed her carry-on bags before her. She hung the larger one on her shoulder and looked through the back window. The custom-made wedding dress laid there across the backseat of the BMW. It was a strapless silk and lace flow-out with many layers. The embroidery was incredible. It was almost as complex as the bride-to-be herself.

"Okay, girl, it's now or never," she urged herself as she headed forward into her future.

Gabriana took a few deep breaths and closed her eyes. When she reopened them, she tossed the parking ticket that the agent had given her into the wastebasket and made her way through the automated doors.

As Gabriana walked forward, she released every thought. They all fell at her feet. She dropped most of the memories and the names, too, right there on the lanolin blocks that she stepped on and over. The mission was on. The decision was made.

One hour later, Gabriana sat on a United Airlines flight headed to L.A. It was now or never. She turned up the iPod in her ears and closed her eyes." Blame it on me, nigga," she mumbled as she stared forward through glossed-over eyes.

Gabriana left Khali standing at the altar. She was not ready to deal.

Luke 9:62

Jesus replied, "No one who puts his hand to the plow and looks back is fit for the kingdom of God."

*To Be Continued...*ne is disconnected Gabriana wouldnt be able to read the text messages below.

CPSIA information can be obtained at www.ICGtesting.com
Printed in the USA
LVOW050724260911

247842LV00001B/4/P